"I want you," she said, staring into those blue eyes that had once meant everything to her.

He gave her a half grin that stopped her heart and seemed to have a direct link to the most feminine parts of her. "You seem a little surprised by that statement."

"I just want to be here with you, all the way with you. Here and now." She knew she was being cryptic, that he couldn't possibly understand what she meant. And she definitely wasn't about to explain, especially not now.

But Jace just nodded. "Then stay with me, Tiger Lily. Just you and me." He bent down and brought his lips to hers again tenderly.

And she did. For the first time in twelve years, she stayed. Because he wasn't just any man. He was *Jace*.

ARMED RESPONSE

USA TODAY Bestselling Author

JANIE CROUCH

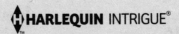

This book is dedicated to my sister-in-law, Kimberly. Thank you
for always being such a source of joy and encouragement,
not just to me, but to everyone around you. And for making
Mark read my books. I love you.

ISBN-13: 978-1-335-63934-9

Armed Response

Copyright © 2018 by Janie Crouch

Recycling programs
for this product may
not exist in your area.

Printed in U.S.A.

Janie Crouch has loved to read romance her whole life. This *USA TODAY* bestselling author cut her teeth on Harlequin Romance novels as a preteen, then moved on to a passion for romantic suspense as an adult. Janie lives with her husband and four children overseas. She enjoys traveling, long-distance running, movie watching, knitting and adventure/obstacle racing. You can find out more about her at janiecrouch.com.

Books by Janie Crouch

Harlequin Intrigue

Omega Sector: Under Siege

Daddy Defender
Protector's Instinct
Cease Fire
Major Crimes
Armed Response

Omega Sector: Critical Response

Special Forces Savior
Fully Committed
Armored Attraction
Man of Action
Overwhelming Force
Battle Tested

Omega Sector

Infiltration
Countermeasures
Untraceable
Leverage

Primal Instinct

Visit the Author Profile page at Harlequin.com.

CAST OF CHARACTERS

Lillian Muir—The sole female member of the Omega Sector SWAT team. Excels in close-quarter combat and marksmanship.

Jace Eakin—Former US Army ranger and temporary member of the Omega Sector SWAT team. An explosives expert.

Ren McClement—Omega Sector founding agent with highest levels of security clearance.

Steve Drackett—Director of the Omega Sector Critical Response Division.

Derek Waterman—Omega Sector SWAT team leader.

Philip Carnell—Temporary member of Omega Sector SWAT team in tactical command.

Saul Poniard—Newest member of Omega Sector SWAT team.

Grace Parker—Omega Sector psychiatrist killed by Damien Freihof a few weeks ago.

Daryl Eakin—Jace's brother who was killed twelve years ago.

Damien Freihof—Terrorist mastermind determined to bring down Omega Sector piece by piece by doing what they did to him: destroying their loved ones.

"Fawkes"—Omega Sector traitor providing inside information to Freihof.

Christina Glasneck—Colorado congresswoman and responsible for the Law Enforcement Systems and Services (LESS) Summit.

Omega Sector—A multi-organizational law-enforcement task force made up of the best agents our country has to offer.

Chapter One

The way some women felt about that perfect little black-dress-and-heels ensemble—ready for anything, able to handle themselves, *bring it on*—Lillian Muir felt about her SWAT cargo pants, combat boots and tactical vest.

The heavy clothing and gear she wore might have felt burdensome at one time on her five-two, one-hundred-pound frame, but she had long since adjusted. Now she almost felt more comfortable with the extra thirty pounds weighing on her than she did with it off. The weight was a comfort. A friend.

Her HK MP5 9mm submachine gun rested against her shoulder, just grazing her chin. Her fingers curled gently around it as she moved through the silent winter air of this Colorado night. A shotgun strapped around her back and a Glock pistol low on one hip provided further assurance she could handle what was ahead.

More than a pair of high heels ever would.

And what was ahead was pissing her the hell off. A man—a *father*—holding his ex-wife and their two children hostage at gunpoint.

"Bulldog One, status."

Lillian tapped the button that allowed her to speak into the communication system attached to her ear under her helmet. "Approaching back door, TC."

"Roger that. Hold for entry." One of the team's newest—and temporary—members, Philip Carnell, was acting as Tactical Command. Carnell wasn't the team's usual TC and his presence added to Lillian's unease about the mission. Not that Carnell wasn't brilliant when it came to planning and calling the shots. He was. Had an IQ of about a million and was able to process tactical information and advantages faster than anyone Lillian had ever seen. His mind was like a damn computer.

But he wasn't part of the usual team. And moreover, he was pretty bitter about that.

They were shorthanded from recent attacks by criminal mastermind Damien Freihof over the past few months. Team members had been hurt and even killed as they battled one assault after another. Explosions. Bullets through windows. Sliced throats. Even assailants at weddings. Freihof had made it his mission in life to wage war on Omega Sector.

Lillian herself had been injured in a mission just two weeks ago, shrapnel from an explosion catching her in the shoulder. She ignored the slight discomfort now. She had bigger things to worry about.

"Bulldog Two, report status," Carnell said.

"I have a visual on the suspect. Single tango. He's pacing. Three hostages. Mom and two kids. All in the kitchen." Bulldog Two's voice was a little too high, too excited. Another person that damn sure wasn't part of the normal elite Omega Sector SWAT team. Damn Damien Freihof and his mole inside Omega.

Lillian ignored that discomfort for now, too.

"I have a shot. Repeat, I have a shot," Bulldog Two said.

Lillian held her tongue. New Kid wasn't her problem.

"Negative, Bulldog Two. Hold your position," Carnell told him.

"I want to take this bastard out," the trainee guy said again. What was his name? Paul?

"Hold, Bulldog Two." This time it was team leader Derek Waterman on the comm unit. He was also out in the darkness surrounding the house.

Lillian's lips pursed. "Derek, request channel change."

"Roger that. Go to channel three, Bulldog One."

Lillian clicked the dial that turned the comm device to a channel so she and the team leader could talk without anyone else listening.

"Go, Lillian," Derek said.

"We going to have a problem with Newbie?"

"His name is Saul. Saul Poniard."

Generally Saul was a good guy. Friendly, surfer-boy looks with a ready smile. He was also pretty excitable, which might have been the reason he was turned down for final SWAT training multiple times. The only reason he was here now was the injuries on the team.

Lillian sighed. "I just don't want him shooting those kids' dad in front of them."

"Roger that," Derek said. "No deadly force unless we have no other options. TC knows that. Carnell won't make that call unless there are no other options and things are escalating."

"I know that. You know that. Just want to make sure New Kid knows that."

Derek grimaced. "Don't worry. I've got him under thumb. I'll pull him out if I need to. Switch channels."

Lillian did so. She'd said her piece, and really didn't have a problem with Saul Poniard except for his excitability, and lack of experience. Derek would handle it. Which was good because she didn't want to have to go take out baby-SWAT wannabe before taking down that scumbag dad on the inside.

Who she could now hear screaming at his wife.

"Tactical Command, this is Bulldog One. I am at the back door. I have visual on the mom and kids but not the tango."

She could see them in the kitchen, the woman and children sitting at a small round wooden table. The mom had both hands reached out toward her children, a boy around nine and a girl around seven, and they sat on either side of her, but not near enough to be touching her.

The tango paced into view, gun in hand, but at least pointing down, and he smacked the mom in the head with his bare hand as he stormed past and out of sight from where Lillian crouched at the window. Guy was still shouting.

"I still have a shot. Repeat, Bulldog Two has a shot," Saul said. He was in a tree on the east side of the house, so Lillian had no doubt the angle gave him a tactical advantage. And yes, if Psycho Dad's actions escalated, then Saul would need to take him out.

But otherwise Lillian would do everything

she could to make sure these kids didn't see a parent—no matter how terrible he was—die right in front of them.

Not here. Not today.

"Negative, Bulldog Two," Philip said. "Bulldog One, can you infiltrate without exposure?"

"Affirmative," Lillian responded. "Especially with all the noise this guy is making."

"Everyone is in position. Go at your discretion," Philip told her. The rest of the team—as well as the new kid—was ready to back her up and take out the tango if needed.

Lillian waited until the guy went on another tirade, screaming right in the mother's ear, both kids sobbing, as an opportunity to slip inside a small crack when she opened the door. The Omega SWAT team regularly used Lillian's small stature to their advantage. This was no different.

She kept to the shadows as she made her way closer to the kitchen.

"Tango is starting to wave the gun again." Saul's voice had reached an excited pitch again. "He's got it to the wife's head."

"Roger that, Bulldog Two. Your shot?"

"Still clear, TC. Just give me the word." Saul was damn near panting with excitement.

Damn it. She'd rather the team take out the father than have the mother die.

"Bulldog One?"

"I have no visual," she muttered.

"Okay, Bulldog Two, you are cleared to—"

Lillian saw movement again in the kitchen. "Hold," she said. "Tango is on the move again. Back to pacing."

"I've still got the shot, TC."

The frustration was evident in Poniard's tone, and Lillian couldn't blame him. Preparing to fire, and being cleared to fire, but then having the order rescinded at the last second, was irritating. But exercising control was also an important part of being a SWAT team member.

"Bulldog One, can you beanbag him?" Carnell asked.

"Roger that, TC. Moving into position." Lillian grinned, replacing her HK MP5 with the shotgun strapped behind her back. The beanbag round was only accurate up to about six meters, but she was within range. Its blow was designed to cause minimal permanent damage while rendering the subject immobile.

The fact that it would hurt Screaming Dad like hell didn't bother Lillian a bit. She crawled forward. She was going to have to pull some sort of Tom Cruise roll-and-shoot nonsense in order to get into position in the quickest way possible. She usually went for much less drama. But not today.

Guy started screaming again. Lillian had had enough.

You want to dance, buddy? We'll dance. Together.

"On my mark," she whispered to the team. "Three, two, one."

Lillian pushed herself from her crouched position in the shadows, twisting her body into a roll as she cleared the wall and came into the opening of the kitchen, landing in a kneel.

She saw surprise light the tango's face. He was swinging his gun around toward her when her finger gently squeezed the trigger on the shotgun, her aim perfect.

The beanbag round hit him square in the chest, propelling him back through the air and away from the table and hostages. The gun fell out of his hand.

Less than two seconds later Lillian was on the tango and the rest of the team was filing through the door, grabbing the children and wife and leading them to safety.

Screaming Dad groaned as Lillian grabbed his hands to cuff them. "Tango is secure."

"You're a woman!" The man's outrage couldn't be more clear.

Lillian arched a single eyebrow. "Yeah? Well, you're an idiot. Turn over."

"I think you done broke my ribs."

Lillian didn't give a rat's ass whether this jerk had a couple of cracked ribs. He was lucky Philip hadn't turned the trigger-happy new kid loose on him. "Shut up. I'll break more than your ribs."

Within a few more minutes the perp was loaded into the back of a squad car and the wife and kids were handed over to the paramedics.

"Nice work, everyone," Derek said over their comm unit. "Let's get packed up and back to HQ to debrief."

Lillian bumped fists with everyone as they made it back to the car. Even Saul, who was smiling like an idiot. Everybody was walking away today. No one seriously injured, even the tango.

That made today a good day.

"Beers on me," Derek said.

That made it an even better day.

LATER THAT NIGHT after the debriefing and the beers, Damien Freihof sat in an abandoned warehouse across town, staring at "Mr. Fawkes." Damien had made it his mission over the last six months to destroy Omega Sector, piece by piece, in payment for taking the life of his beloved wife.

Fawkes, as he so cleverly liked to be called, had proven very useful over the last few months in that endeavor. Fawkes's inside information on Omega had been quite helpful indeed.

Fawkes still wouldn't give Damien his real name. Damien wondered how upsetting it would be to the younger man to know that Damien had figured it out weeks ago. The man might be brilliant, but Damien didn't work with people he didn't know.

Damien's and Fawkes's ideologies were different. Fawkes looked to destroy and rebuild all of law enforcement. Damien just wanted Omega to suffer the way he did when he'd lost his Natalie. Wanted them to know what it meant to experience unbearable loss.

But if Damien could bring chaos across the country by destroying the foundation of all law enforcement, as was Fawkes's plan, then hell, he was up for that, too.

"It's time," Fawkes said as he paced back and forth hardly visible beside a window, even in the full moon. "You'll be ready, right? We only have eight days."

Damien sat perched against a desk. "Yes, I'll be ready to do my part in your master plan."

"We've gotten rid of two of their team members completely. Another is injured and not fully up to speed." Fawkes continued his pacing.

"It's a mistake to underestimate the Critical

Response Division, even when they're weakened." Damien had learned that the hard way.

"They brought in a new guy on the SWAT team. That was unexpected." Fawkes stopped and studied Damien as he said it, as if gauging his response.

Damien knew all about the new guy. "Is that a problem?"

"No." Fawkes resumed his pacing. "The team thinks they're so smart, but they're not. I've left a trail. It's going to lead right to the very heart of the SWAT team. The sweetheart."

"Lillian Muir?" Damien raised an eyebrow.

"I've got special plans for her. Have already left clues in the system that lead back to her as the mole I know they're searching for."

Damien had to admit Fawkes's computer skills were impressive. He'd provided information that had helped Damien a great deal. Most particularly two weeks ago, when Omega had almost captured him at his own house. Without a warning from Fawkes, Damien would never have made it out.

Nor taken one of the SWAT team out of action in the process.

Fawkes might not be the easiest person to work with, but he definitely knew how to manipulate a computer system. And how to manipulate people, for that matter. People didn't take him seriously enough, including those at Omega Sector.

Which was probably why he was trying to blow up—*literally*—all of law enforcement.

Or maybe he just had mommy issues. Whatever. Damien didn't care why Fawkes was doing it, he just wanted to see Omega Sector destroyed. If Lillian Muir was going to take the fall for that, even better. Damien would do a little checking up on her himself.

Fawkes wasn't the only one with computer skills and digging-up-info skills.

"Is there even going to be anyone left to search for the villain after you get through next week?" Damien asked.

Fawkes stilled. "I'll be left. I will be one of the few tactically trained agents left in the whole agency. Hell, in the whole country. And all the destruction will lead right to Lillian Muir's door. She'll be dead and unable to open the door, but the destruction and blame will still lead right to her."

Damien grinned. One thing Fawkes had was exuberance. "Sounds like a perfect plan to me."

Chapter Two

Jace Eakin stretched his long legs out in front of him in an office chair that probably hadn't been comfortable even when it was new. Now that it was ratty and at least a dozen years past that, it was even less so. His knee was stiff from too many hours cramped in a plane, his shoulder vaguely ached from a bullet he'd taken years ago in Afghanistan. Thirty-two was too young to feel this old.

He was in an office that looked like it was out of some old gumshoe movie, complete with dirty windows and low ceilings. The man sitting behind a desk looked almost as rumpled as the office itself.

Jace knew Ren McClement was anything but.

Jace had first met him ten years ago when they served together in the US Army Rangers in the Middle East. Working side by side with someone in daily life-or-death situations

showed that person's true colors. Ren Mc-
Clement was one of the few people in the world
Jace trusted without restriction. He knew the
feeling was mutual. Which was why he was
here now in this godforsaken seat in some out-
of-the-way office in Washington, DC, rather
than putting the finishing touches on his ranch
in Colorado.

"Ren, seriously, dude, you've got to get some
chairs not built for midgets."

Both Ren and the other man in the room,
Steve Drackett, chuckled. Ren had gotten out
of the army not long after the time he spent in
Afghanistan with Jace. Because of his skills
and security clearance, Ren had immediately
been brought into Omega Sector, a joint task
force made up of the best agents the United
States had to offer.

Jace knew Ren was one of the highest-rank-
ing members of Omega, and that he worked
mostly in covert missions.

Nothing surprising about that. Ren had had
the ability to blend in with almost any situation
even back in his Ranger days. That the government was smart enough to use him for clandes-
tine work wasn't surprising to Jace.

What was a mystery to him was why Ren
had asked *him* here to begin with. Although
always happy to see his old friend, Jace was

not an Omega Sector agent. He wasn't an agent at all.

"Yeah, budget for this place wasn't very big," Ren said. "Not that I'm in here enough to worry about that anyway."

Ren could probably have a very high-end government office with a million-dollar view of DC, but chose not to. Jace knew for a fact that Ren never entered a government building unless he had to, and even then it wasn't through the front door. The undercover nature of his job prohibited it.

"I can see why you wouldn't want to be here often. And speaking of, why am *I* here? I'm assuming there's a reason other than reliving old times."

Ren nodded. "We have a situation in the Omega Critical Response Division out in Colorado Springs. A mole who is leaking information to a terrorist named Damien Freihof. We know the mole is someone inside the SWAT team. Steve—" he gestured to the other man, who was leaning with one shoulder against the wall "—has requested that I send in someone I trust to help find the mole."

Steve pushed himself away from the wall and handed Jace a thin file with some papers inside. "We found this Manifesto of Change document hidden in one of our Omega computer servers."

On my honor, I will never betray my badge, my integrity, my character or the public trust.

I will always have the courage to hold myself and others accountable for our actions.

I will always uphold the constitution, my community and the agency I serve.

Jace looked over at Ren, then Steve. "This looks like some sort of law-enforcement creed."

Steve nodded. "It's the oath of honor that law enforcement officers take at their swearing-in ceremony. But keep reading."

We all took an oath to uphold the law, but instead we have allowed the public to make a mockery of it. Where is the honor, the integrity, the character in not using the privilege and power given to us by our training and station to wipe clean those who would infect our society? We were meant to rise up, to be an example to the people, to control them when needed in order to make a more perfect civilization.

But we are weak. Afraid of popular opinion whenever force must be used. So now we have changed the configuration of law enforcement forever.

And now, only now, will you truly understand what it means to hold yourselves accountable for your actions. Only with death is life truly appreciated. Only with violence can true change be propagated. As we build anew, let us not make the same mistakes. Let the badge mean something again.

Let the badge rule as it was meant to do.

Jace shifted slightly in his chair. "Okay, I'll admit, this is scary. And I sympathize, I really do, that this has come from within your own organization, but I'm not an agent. There's got to be other people you trust who could do a better job than I could."

Ren glanced over at Steve and then back at Jace. "We're not looking for someone long-term. This is a time-sensitive op."

Steve nodded. "I would've bet my life that the traitor was not one of my SWAT team members. I've known most of those people for years. But intel has suggested that not only is the mole a member of SWAT, but also has a plan that will involve a massive loss of life."

"Do you have details about how? When?" Jace asked.

Steve nodded. "Within the next two weeks. Our strong suspicions are that it has to do with a law-enforcement summit scheduled in Denver next week. It will have police chiefs and politicians in attendance from all over the country."

"That would definitely make a good target." Jace looked back at Ren. "And if you need an extra hand with a rifle, I'm more than willing to help out, especially since I'm headed out to Colorado anyway."

"Still planning on breeding and raising dogs?" Ren asked. "Horses? Opening your ranch?"

"Hey, don't mock my dream." Jace had always wanted to own a small parcel of land where he could raise animals, particularly dogs, that could be trained for service members and veterans who suffered from PTSD. Maybe even make it into a place where vets could come and enjoy space and quiet for a temporary stay when they needed it.

Jace had made some savvy financial investments in his twenties that had given him the means to make this dream a reality now. He'd be able to cover himself financially until he was able to make a living from his business. He was looking forward to working outside, with the land and animals. He also looked forward to not having to be constantly worried about being in danger.

Although risk cognizance had been a part

of his life for so long it was second nature to him now.

"I wouldn't dream of mocking it." Ren smiled. "Hell, I may be joining you before this is all over. But I was hoping you would help me out before you got out of the game for good."

"We don't need an agent," Steve said. "We just need someone who can come in and pass for a SWAT team member. Somebody who has the qualifications and physical prowess to join the team. Because of attacks by Damien Freihof, we're down a couple of members, so bringing in someone from the outside wouldn't be unheard of."

"And then once I'm in there?"

"Then there's one person particularly under suspicion who we need you to get close to." Ren leaned forward on his desk, watching Jace closely. "Lillian Muir."

The name had Jace actually rising from his seat before he even knew it.

"Lillian Muir?" He looked from Ren to Steve. "Lillian Muir is a member of the Omega Sector SWAT team?"

"Not only a member, one of the *best* members. One of the most gifted SWAT personnel I've ever known," Steve said.

Jace began pacing back and forth behind the chair he'd just vacated.

Lillian Muir.

He'd be lying if he said he hadn't wondered what had happened to her over the years. He hadn't seen her in twelve years, since he was twenty and she was eighteen. The day they were supposed to leave to join the army together, to get out of a pretty rotten living situation in Tulsa. To figure out their future together, which for Jace had always meant marriage as soon as he could talk her into it.

He hadn't seen her since the day he'd found her in his brother's arms.

Jace looked at Ren. "You know, of course, that Lillian and I have a history."

Ren nodded. "You and I talked about a woman you cared about a great deal back when we served together. And you'd mentioned her name was Lillian. When I found out the Omega Lillian was the same as your Lillian, I thought we could kill two birds with one trusted stone."

Jace shook his head. "You also know things didn't end well between the two of us. I'm probably not the most neutral person. She decided she'd rather have my brother than me."

Daryl had died in a fire not long after Jace joined the army, but that didn't change the fact that Lillian had chosen Daryl, not him.

"I just want to say officially and on the record that I do not think Lillian is the mole,"

Steve said, conviction clear in his voice. "As a matter of fact, I'm hoping you'll be able to come in and clear her."

"Clear her? Why me? There's got to be someone better."

"It's a perfect storm of problems," Ren said. "We need someone we can trust. We need someone who has the skills to infiltrate a SWAT team. And we need someone Lillian may be willing to get close to."

Jace shrugged. "The first two I might fit. But Lillian won't get close to me. There's got to be someone else. Friend. Boyfriend. Somebody."

"I recruited Lillian basically off the streets nine years ago." Steve shook his head. "She's got a tactical awareness and physical control of her body that has only improved over the years with training and education. But, despite being an excellent team member, Lillian has never gotten close to anyone since I've known her."

Jace scrubbed a hand over his face. "Even more reason why she's not going to get close to me. Some people are just lone wolves."

Jace knew enough about Lillian's upbringing to not be surprised that she kept to herself. She wasn't ever going to be the life of the party. But never having gotten close to *anyone*? The two of them had been plenty close at one time. Or so he'd thought.

"Our division psychiatrist was killed by Freihof two weeks ago," Steve continued. "Her case files are confidential, even with her death. But I do know for a fact that Lillian was seeing Dr. Parker regularly. And Dr. Parker believed there was a sexual trauma of some kind in Lillian's history."

Ren leaned back in his chair. "Honestly, we were hoping maybe you knew something about that and could use it to foster a closeness between the two of you."

"I don't. If that happened, it happened after she and I…separated." Jace grimaced, tension creeping through his body. Despite her leaving him for his brother, Jace would never have wished something like that on her. Couldn't stand the thought of someone hurting her that way.

"Like I said, I don't have any details. And it may not even be accurate. But I know Dr. Parker had suggested that finding someone from her past, someone she knew before the trauma, might be the key to helping her overcome it." Steve gestured toward Jace. "Maybe you could be that person. Help us find the real mole. Help her work through whatever is in her history."

"What if she is the real mole?" Jace asked. He didn't want to believe it. He *didn't* believe it. But it could still be the truth. He'd known her twelve years ago and she cheated on him. Had that developed into even darker tendencies as she'd gotten older?

Steve took a step forward. "She's not."

Ren held his hands out in front of him in a soothing gesture. "Steve, you're too close to this. You know you are."

Jace jerked his chin at Steve. "You involved with Lillian?"

"No, happily married and a new father." Steve's eyes narrowed. "Plus, did you not just hear what I said about her not getting close to people? That particularly goes for men."

Jace shrugged, studying Steve with hooded eyes. "Thought maybe you might be the exception to that."

"Steve cares about the entire team," Ren insisted. "He wants to catch Freihof and the mole more than anyone else, especially given the people they've lost. And the mole doesn't know that we're on to him. Or her, as it may be. So we want to use that to our advantage.

Steve poking around will draw attention. Not to mention he's not neutral."

Jace sat back down in the uncomfortable chair. "And you think I am?"

Ren stared him down. "I think I would trust you with my life—and have—multiple times over. I think you have an innate situational awareness that was only honed in your years as a Ranger. I think you will be fresh eyes and able to pinpoint specifics others may have missed."

Ren leaned back in his chair but didn't lose eye contact as he continued. "And I think this is a chance for you to finally put your history with Lillian to rest and move on. She's not the only one who hasn't gotten close to anyone else in the last twelve years."

Jace was also a loner. Lillian hadn't had anything to do with his choice not to settle down with anyone. But that was irrelevant to the situation at hand.

Ren was right—it was time to leave Lillian Muir behind for good.

"Fine. I'll do it. Another couple of weeks isn't going to change my plans for the ranch. I just hope I'm able to do what you guys think I can."

Ren nodded. "Your best has never once not been good enough."

Jace just shrugged. That wasn't true. They'd

lost men in the line of duty whom Jace wished he could bring back. "I appreciate the sentiment."

Steve stepped up and shook his hand. "Welcome to the team."

Chapter Three

Lillian had been quick and wiry her whole life. Not just fast with running, although she could average a six-minute mile for ten miles in a row, but swift with everything. Her hand movements, her body movements, how she processed info.

A lot of it probably came from early in her life, when if she wanted to eat, she'd had to steal food from the grocery store or local market. And if she wanted to sleep safely, away from her mother's drunken wrath or boyfriends' wandering hands, she'd learned how to move quickly and silently out the window.

Those lessons might have been hard to come by, but each of them had made her into the woman—the *warrior*—she was today.

Whatever didn't kill her had better start running.

The SWAT team was sparring and doing some general workouts in the training area until the new guy got there. *Another* new guy. Evidently this one had a little more experience than Saul, the friendly yet trigger-happy newbie who had been filling in for the last couple of weeks. Or anybody was better than Philip Carnell, the computer whiz who had been working with them as an analyst in hostile situations for the last two months.

Carnell had a mind like a steel trap, but the personality of a horse's ass. Which was probably an insult to the hind end of a horse. Nobody liked Philip and he had a bone to pick with everybody about seemingly every damn thing. Lillian avoided him whenever possible. Hell, everybody avoided him whenever possible, unless he was acting as Tactical Command, as he had been a couple of days ago. Carnell was great at finding fast solutions in dangerous tactical situations, but he wasn't physically adept enough to be a part of the tactical team.

He'd only sulked about that fact and gave his opinion about "the unfairness of elitist practices" of the SWAT team about once every hour. Lillian was glad to not have to deal with him in training or in the field.

Saul wasn't so bad. He tried to get a little too friendly, and grinned a little too much for her taste. But at least Surfer Boy didn't make her want to lock him in a trunk, like she did with Carnell.

Right now she brought her leg around in a vicious roundhouse kick and hit the punching bag. Roman Weber, her teammate holding the bag for her, took a quick step back.

"Trying to take out all your aggression on one poor defenseless piece of canvas?" He chuckled as he grabbed the bag more firmly.

"Too many new people, Roman. I don't like change."

"Oh, yeah? Try finding out you're about to be a dad. Now, *that's* change."

Lillian grinned at him. "Yeah, every time that happens to me I swear it's not gonna happen again."

Despite his wounds from an explosion two months ago, she knew Roman couldn't be happier about Keira being back in his life and the baby they had on the way. Hell, it seemed like just about everybody on the SWAT team had found romance-novel-type true love within the last year.

Lillian was thrilled for them, she really was. She liked each and every one of the women her teammates had fallen for. But love and marriage weren't in the cards for her. She'd long since accepted that. Emotional attachment just wasn't her thing.

But she had a career she savored and kicked ass at. That was enough.

"I hear this new guy is actually qualified to be on the team. An Army Ranger. Steve Drackett vouches for him personally," Roman said.

Lillian punched the bag again. "I just wish Liam was back in action." Their teammate had almost been killed by a biological weapon three weeks ago.

"He's alive and going to recover. That's what matters."

Omega Sector's casualty list at Damien Freihof's hand was getting too damn long.

Liam Goetz, SWAT team member: seriously injured via chemical inhalation. Hospitalized two weeks.

Roman Weber, SWAT team member: seriously injured via explosion. In a coma for more than a week.

Tyrone Marcus, SWAT team member-in-training: killed in action via explosion.

Grace Parker, Omega psychiatrist: murdered in cold blood.

And those were just the worst of the worst.

Especially Grace. *Damn it.* Lillian forced herself to push away the grief that threatened to suck her under at the thought of losing the other woman and the close friend she had become.

She switched with Roman and held the bag as

he went through a series of kicks and punches, at a slower speed and with less force because of his recent injuries. As soon as the new guy came in, they'd be doing some training with him. Running the SWAT obstacle course, some sparring, throwing him immediately into the mix.

"Hopefully this new guy won't crush on you like Saul," Roman said between punches.

She rolled her eyes. "Yeah. I don't think Saul understands that I don't date work people."

"You don't date anyone."

This was an old argument. "I do date. I just don't announce it around here like all you lovesick fools. There's enough swooning going on around here without adding me to the mix."

"I'd like to meet a boyfriend of yours just once."

Lillian took her turn at the bag. "Fine. I'll bring the next one around for approval, okay?"

She wouldn't. Roman was right, she didn't have boyfriends. She had sex with random guys, probably too often, but she tended to check out mentally in the middle of the act itself. Then immediately left afterward. Not being able to remember any part of the sexual act did not lend itself toward building a relationship.

She and Grace Parker had been working on

some of Lillian's issues before Grace had died. Lillian's triggers. The fact that she'd *never* been able to have sex and remember it clearly afterward.

Disassociation due to acute sexual trauma. That was what Grace had told Lillian was the clinical term for it. And that it was treatable. That they would continue to work together so that Lillian's mind didn't try to escape every time she became intimate with someone. They'd made progress over the last year.

And now Grace was dead.

Lillian attacked the punching bag with renewed vigor. "I just want SWAT to be ready for when we get the call to go take out Freihof. I'll even date the new guy if he can help us be ready for that."

Roman chuckled. "Hell, *I'll* date the new guy if he can help with that."

"I'm sure Keira won't mind, considering Freihof nearly got her killed."

"If Steve vouches for this guy, then that's all I need to know," Roman said.

Lillian trusted Steve completely also. "Yeah, me, too. What's the guy's name? I promise I'll make an effort at learning it."

"Jace Eakin."

Lillian's head snapped up and she glared at Roman, about to make him repeat the name.

Roman gestured to the door. "Here he is."

It could not possibly be. There was no way. She turned, slowly. No. Way.

Yes way.

"Jace. Jace Eakin," she whispered.

"You know him?"

"I did. A long, long time ago."

She felt like her heart had completely stopped beating. *Jace* was the new guy? Part of her wasn't surprised that he was qualified. He'd been strong, fast and smart when she knew him twelve years ago. Evidently the army had turned him into someone even more dangerous.

And he was particularly dangerous for her. He knew every secret she'd gone to such lengths to keep hidden from the team. He knew how she used to steal and run illegal items all over town for the gang they'd both been in. She'd been fast, trustworthy and had looked innocent. She'd never once gotten caught.

Jace Eakin knew every secret she'd made sure no one else at Omega Sector knew.

Except one. And he would never know that one.

She kept him in her peripheral vision as she returned to her assault on the punching bag.

"If you know him, don't you want to go talk to him?" Roman asked, grabbing the bag.

She shook her head. It was all she could do to

not run from the room. And Lillian was known for not running from anything.

She saw Jace put his bag on the floor and talk to Derek. A few minutes later he was headed toward the locker room.

Fifteen minutes after that Derek was calling the entire team together, including Jace.

"Everybody, this is Jace Eakin. Eakin, the team." Derek looked around at everyone. "They'll all introduce themselves individually."

So far Jace had avoided looking at her directly, but Lillian had no doubt he was aware of her presence. She could almost feel his awareness of her.

The same way she was aware of him.

"Jace is coming in to help us with the Law Enforcement Systems and Services Summit next week in Denver," Derek continued. "The LESS Summit, as everyone knows, is going to bring in the bigwigs from all over the country. Our job is to provide internal protection for that event."

Ashton Fitzgerald, team sharpshooter and general smart-ass, spoke up. "LESS is more."

Everybody echoed Ashton's statement, the slogan for LESS, as they always did. LESS was a system that would link together law-enforcement-agency computers all over the country, providing valuable instant connectivity and the ability to share data.

"Denver is also expecting a number of demonstrators and protesters, so if needed, we'll help out with that. Everybody knows we're a little undermanned right now. Roman and Lillian are both coming off injuries. Jace is joining us as temporary replacement for Liam. Saul is also going to be joining us as a full member for the LESS Summit."

Everyone was quiet at those words. Building the cohesion needed for the team to run smoothly in just a week wasn't going to be easy. Lillian shifted restlessly. She wasn't the only one.

Derek looked at each one of them. "You're angry at Damien Freihof. All of us are angry after what happened to Grace Parker, not to mention our team. We all want to get our hands on Freihof and make him pay. And that time is coming. But our focus right now is on the LESS Summit. It's about keeping those attending safe. So I want everyone to stay frosty and focused. We have a job to do."

Lillian raised her hand halfway. "What about the rumor that there's a mole inside Omega providing Freihof intel?"

She wanted to nail that traitor bastard just as much as she wanted to nail Freihof.

"I know a mole is suspected," Derek responded. "But to date, no official evidence has been found to support that rumor. We all know Freihof loves to play head games. Getting us to turn on each other, go on witch hunts, is exactly what he wants. So we're not going to do that. If you see anything suspicious, you report it to me, but we don't go around accusing each other of anything."

Lillian nodded. She glanced over and found Jace openly studying her. Their eyes met and she was determined not to look away first. Jace, damn his still gorgeous blue eyes, seemed to have the same determination.

Derek saved them both from their battle of wills.

"We're going to get into training immediately to get us working as a team. And this week we're going to put in long, team-building hours." Derek turned to Jace, who had changed into workout clothes from the khakis and collared shirt he'd arrived in. "Eakin, although you come recommended from a man we all highly respect, if you don't mind, we'd like to see what you're capable of."

Jace nodded. "You'd be a fool not to."

Lillian froze at the sound of Jace's voice. The deep timbre still did something to her. Nudged at parts of her that had been sleeping so long she'd thought they were dead. The most feminine parts of her. For a moment she couldn't breathe as her mind attempted to figure out what she was feeling.

Desire.

It had been so long—twelve years, in fact—since she'd felt clear, untainted desire for a man.

And she was feeling it for the man who, with just a sentence or two about her past, could destroy the rapport she'd taken years to build with her team and probably cost her her job.

Omega Sector generally frowned upon employing people who were once part of an unofficial gang in the streets of Tulsa. While their gang hadn't had turf wars and drive-bys, she'd definitely broken the law multiple times throughout her teenage years.

"We'll hit the team obstacle course this afternoon," Derek continued. "But I thought we'd begin with some sparring."

"Sounds good to me." That deep voice again.

"Who would you like to start with?"

Jace's full lips were turned up at one corner as if he knew some private joke. "Why don't you just pair me with your best close-quarters fighter and I'll go from there."

Everybody chuckled at the new guy's guts.

Even Derek smiled. "Even better, why don't

you tell me who *you* think our best close-quarters fighter is?"

Surely Jace would pick Roman or Derek. Both of them were big—over six feet tall with biceps the size of tree trunks.

Lillian could take down both of them. Had done so, in fact. She was pretty damn fast, stronger than she looked, and had spent the last twelve years making sure no man—no matter what his size—would be able to force her to do something she didn't want to do.

Never again.

"Sure." Jace looked at everyone around the circle, as people started stretching and warming up while listening. "There's a number of people who I think could give me a run for my money. But if I had to guess who's most capable of kicking someone's ass, I think it would be this one."

He pointed straight at Lillian.

She could hear the soft chuckles of her teammates, and felt Roman pat her on the shoulder. They didn't know why Jace had chosen her. Because he really thought she was the best close-quarters fighter? Because he thought she'd be easy to take down? She wasn't.

Damn it, she didn't want this. Didn't want to touch Jace Eakin in any way. But she'd never been one to back down from a fight.

She wasn't going to start now.

Stretching her shoulders, she put on the sparring mask and gloves and met Jace in the sparring ring. They gave each other a brief nod and then began.

They spent the first couple of minutes dancing around each other, throwing a jab here and a few kicks there. Lillian felt herself loosening up. She excelled at close-quarters combat. Her body knew what to do from muscle memory.

Jace got a little more serious, sending a spinning back kick in the direction of her head. She dropped low and hooked the back of her leg behind his, bringing him to the mat with a thud.

For just a moment they were face-to-face near the floor.

"I taught you that move," he whispered.

She leaped up to her feet and he followed, pushing off from his shoulder and straight onto his feet.

Lillian didn't let him get resituated. She used her greatest advantage—her speed—and flew at him with a series of punches and kicks. Jace was forced to go on the defensive, and did a damn good job of it.

She stepped back as he nearly backed out of bounds, ending her attack. "You didn't teach me that."

He grinned. "I sure as hell didn't. Impressive." Without warning he came at her, forcing her to go on the defensive this time.

All in all, they were pretty evenly matched. Derek eventually called the match to a halt when it became apparent neither of them was going to win easily. "Let's save some energy for the rest of today's training. There's a lot of hours still left."

Jace took off his gloves and held his hand out to shake hers. "Nice job, Tiger Lily. Although I'm not surprised."

You could've heard a grasshopper karate-chop a fly. *Tiger Lily.* Nobody ever called her Lily, not if they expected to live to see the next sunrise. And no one had ever called her Tiger Lily—the beautiful and exotic flower—but Jace. Hearing the words did something to her she couldn't explain and didn't want to delve into too closely.

So she kept her cool.

"Welcome to the team, Jace. And it's Lillian. Just Lillian, nothing else."

Chapter Four

"Lily, hold up."

He smiled as he saw her shoulders stiffen at the name. Her curt instructions on the sparring mat not to call her anything but Lillian had just spurred his desire to call her by her old nickname.

But it was her whispered words as they had left the sparring area that had really caught his attention.

Don't say anything about who we were.

Jace wasn't sure if that meant their personal history or the gang-related activities they'd participated in during their youth. She might not have ever told anyone about that, especially the latter. Since she had never been arrested, nor had he, it wasn't in either of their permanent records. She didn't have to worry about him spilling her secret. Not that one anyway.

Working with her today, fighting with her, seeing how everyone else interacted with her…

Jace couldn't help being impressed. She had taken all the natural physical skills she'd had as a teenager—speed, flexibility, sheer grit— and had formed herself into nothing short of a warrior.

He'd known it from the first punch she'd thrown in the sparring ring. She'd always been feisty, but now she was deadly. Small but fierce.

She'd been the only woman in the room or on the field, and that hadn't seemed to bother her at all. The men hadn't treated her any differently than they treated each other. Even with their limitations because of injuries, the team members had relied on and functioned around each other's strengths.

No point in Lillian being the one on the bottom hoisting her teammates up the fifteen-foot wall that was part of the obstacle course. Could she have done it if she needed to? Jace had no doubt. But it wasn't her specialty, so instead the team had sent her up and over first. Nobody in this close-knit group played politics: you weren't given an assignment just because you were a man or a woman, you were given an assignment because of your strengths and talents.

Part of the course had also involved an underground tube, which there was no way in hell Jace was ever going to fit through. Neither were most of the men on the team. But Lillian had no problem. So she was sent.

Again, nothing to do with gender, everything to do with what was best for the team.

The men respected her, she respected them. Even the outsiders, the couple of guys besides Jace who obviously weren't regular members of the team, respected her.

And Jace would bet his next paycheck that everything Steve Drackett had said was true. Lillian had not been intimate with any of these men. There was no flash of recognition, no secret smiles...

No nicknames that had been only for them twelve years before. Like Jace had just said to her again.

"I told you, it's Lillian now. Not Lily. Nobody ever called me that but you anyway. And definitely not Tiger Lily."

He jogged the rest of the way to catch up with her. "Old habits. You know how it is."

"It's not like you've been saying my name very often in the past twelve years, so it shouldn't be too difficult for you to make the change."

"I'll do my best." He held his hand up with his fingers open in Mr. Spock's Vulcan *V* symbol. "Scout's honor."

She thawed minutely. "Jackass." She shook

her head. "You were never a Boy Scout *or* a Vulcan."

And he wasn't going to stop calling her Lily, either.

They reached her car, a gray Honda Civic. About as unflashy a vehicle that was made. She opened the trunk and set her duffel bag inside. Then turned to him.

"Why are you here, Jace?"

Giving her as much truth as he could was probably his best option. "Ren McClement asked me. He and I served in the army together for a few years. You know him?"

She shrugged. "Not personally. But everyone knows *of* him. He's pretty much an Omega Sector legend."

"Steve Drackett and Ren said the team needed someone with experience who could jump right in. To help with this LESS Summit thing." Jace looked over to where some of the others were coming out of the building. "No offense, but your team is a little shaky right now. And the two new guys are not exactly anything to write home about."

Lillian rubbed her fingers against her forehead. "That's for damn sure."

"Carnell doesn't play well with anyone. And that guy Saul Poniard is a little too flippant for my taste. That could be disastrous in a lot of situations."

"I agree. Steve recognizes it, too, but right now we don't have a lot of options."

He took a slight step closer to her, unable to stop himself. "Exactly. Ren knows me and knows he can trust me. And you guys needed someone with my skill set."

Talking coming from the parking lot caught their attention and Jace took a step back. They both waved to the other members of the team as they got in their vehicles one by one.

"And did you know I would be here when you said yes to Ren?" Lillian finally asked as her teammates drove away.

This was a much trickier question to answer. He knew he shouldn't have any qualms about lying to her. After all, she had been the completely dishonest one all those years ago. But he found the thought of telling her lies to be more difficult than he expected.

"Ren mentioned there was someone else here from Tulsa. A Lillian. But I couldn't be one-hundred-percent sure that it was you. You were impressive out there today, Tiger Lily."

She glared at him but didn't press the nick-name issue. "Thanks."

"Seriously. You can handle yourself. I mean,

you've always been able to handle yourself, but this was so much more than that."

Lillian leaned back against her car but didn't meet his eyes. "Thanks. You, too. Of course, I'm not surprised or anything. You were always built like a military man. Physically and mentally. I guess you just honed that over the years. So you got out?"

He nodded. "Yeah. For almost a year now. I loved the army, but it was time."

"Moving back to Tulsa?"

"No. Nothing for me there anymore. I actually bought some land here in Colorado. I'm opening a ranch of sorts."

Her brown eyes got big. "A ranch? I didn't know you had any interest in animals."

"I didn't, really, not when you knew me before. Not that there was much space for animals in downtown Tulsa anyway. But we had bomb dogs when I served over in the Middle East. Really found I had a love for them. So I'll be raising them and some other animals. Working with vets, too."

Hopefully providing people with PTSD a place to come and heal for a little while when things got to be too much.

"That sounds amazing. I'm glad your experience in the military was a good one."

"You would've done well in the military,

too." The words were out of his mouth before he could stop them. Lillian should've gone into the military with him. That had been their plan. The military had catered to both of their strengths.

Now she *really* wouldn't look at him. "Yeah. I always thought so."

He had to decide right now whether to battle this out—what had happened between her and his brother—or leave it alone. He didn't want to fight with her the entire time he was here— that would be counterproductive to his ultimate mission of getting closer to her—but he didn't want to leave Daryl as the elephant constantly in the room between them.

He leaned in just slightly closer to her. "Twelve years was a long time ago. I think it's safe to let bygones be bygones, right?"

Now her brown eyes peered up at him. "Yeah, I'm sure that's true."

"And if it means anything, I'm sorry Daryl passed away so soon after the two of you got together. I don't know if it would've lasted or whatever, but I'm sorry you didn't get the chance to find out."

Jace had never seen the blood drain from someone's face so quickly. Lillian's slight weight fell back more heavily against her car.

Jace couldn't help himself. He reached toward her. "Are you okay?"

Did the thought of Daryl's death still hit her so hard?

"Daryl and I would never have made it as a couple." Her laugh was bitter. "If there's one thing I'm sure about, that's it."

She pushed herself away from the car and he could almost see her withdraw into herself. Part of him wanted to press, but on the other hand, he *really* did not want to know intimate details about her relationship with his brother.

She turned and reached for the car door, opening it. Jace took a step closer, boxing her in.

They both felt it. The attraction between them. Daryl or not, it was still there. It had been buzzing around them all day, and now it was pooling in the air between them.

It didn't matter about twelve years, it didn't matter about Daryl, it didn't matter that they didn't know enough about each other now to be sure if they even liked each other.

The heat was still there, just like it had always been.

"You need to talk to Ren," she finally said, her back to him.

With his hand on the frame of her door and the other on the roof of her car, she was, in essence, trapped in his arms. If she turned around, it would almost be like in an embrace.

But she didn't turn as she continued. "Tell Ren this won't work. Help him find someone else."

"Why do I make you so uncomfortable, Tiger Lily? You're the one who gave me up, remember? And like we said, it was over a decade ago. It shouldn't matter now."

She shook her head with a little jerk. "It'll be easier for both of us if you're not here."

"Since when have you or I ever done anything the easy way? We are a good team. You had to have seen that out there today."

She nodded stiffly. Jace took a step forward, which caused Lillian to turn around. Suddenly all he could see was her mouth.

Cursing himself, he brought his lips down to hers. He couldn't help himself, it was like being caught in some tractor beam from a science fiction movie.

Her lips were as soft as he remembered. As sweet. Sweeter, if possible.

She held herself stiffly for the first few seconds, as he teased her lips slowly, nibbling at them, but then he felt her give in. She sighed as if she couldn't fight it, either.

Her fingers slid into his hair, pulling him closer, and a sound of hunger left him, his mouth moving more hungrily on hers, their tongues twining. The attraction and heat pushed at them in waves.

When Jace finally stepped back, they both just stared at each other. Then, without another word, Lily got in her car and started it, pulling away so quickly that if he hadn't stepped back she might've run over his toes. All he could do was watch her drive away.

He muttered a curse under his breath. He'd been sent here to do a job, get more info, find out if Lillian had anything to do with this mole. Not kiss her senseless within the first few hours of his being back in the same general vicinity as her.

He'd counted on his sense of betrayal to help him keep his distance from her. To be able to remain objective and even cold.

Jace should've known better. He'd been many things around Lillian Muir, but cold was never one of them.

Seven hours into this mission and already things had become a hell of a lot more complicated.

Chapter Five

Showing up at Omega HQ the next day knowing Jace would be part of the team, part of her inner circle after twelve years of not having seen him at all, was pretty much inconceivable to Lillian.

And the fact that they'd made out yesterday? She couldn't even wrap her head around that. She didn't make out with people. Making out was for teenagers.

And she especially didn't make out in the Damn. Parking. Lot. Sure, the entire team had left by then, but still. What would people say if someone had seen her lip-locked with the new guy just a few hours after meeting him?

After the Tiger Lily comment, plus the fact that she'd mentioned it to Roman, everyone had heard or figured out she and Jace had a history. But that still didn't account for her sucking face with him.

And hell if heat didn't course through her

at that thought. Again. Like it had done all night long.

Lillian had a lot of sleepless nights. But never had they involved being so caught up thinking about a kiss that she couldn't get to sleep. It was like something out of a Sweet Valley High novel.

She wished she could call Grace about it. Get her opinion as both psychiatrist and woman. Although she knew what Grace would tell her.

To take a chance. To be willing to leave herself unguarded for once.

But Lillian couldn't call Grace. Because Freihof had killed her.

That was enough to wipe all thoughts of teen-romance-books-style kisses out of her mind. Jace was here for a purpose. That purpose had nothing to do with Lillian and everything to do with keeping the LESS Summit safe, especially if Freihof decided to make some sort of play.

She would do well to remember that.

Jace Eakin was now, at least temporarily, taking up residence in her home—Omega HQ was much more home than the one-bedroom apartment that basically just housed her stuff. She would work with him. Get him up to speed. Keep it strictly professional. Definitely no more kissing.

In the locker room she changed out of her civilian clothes and into her training fatigues. She arrived in the SWAT station house living room thirty minutes before she was scheduled to be there. Derek was already there sitting at the conference table that took up a good section of the room, looking over paperwork for the team.

Jace was there, too, on the opposite side of the room.

Ignoring Jace, she walked over to Derek and sat down next to him. Derek slid a file over to her.

"Today's schedule."

Nothing out of the ordinary. Some PT, time to go over the building plans of the LESS Summit and one of Lillian's favorite drills.

"The Gauntlet. Haven't done that one in a while. Pretty brutal."

Derek grinned. "I thought it would be a good team-builder. Trial by fire." He glanced over his shoulder. "I'm going to have you pair up with Eakin."

"For the Gauntlet?"

"That and for the summit."

"Seriously?"

Lilian glanced over at Jace, who was leaning against the wall messing with his phone. The slight smirk lifting the corner of his mouth let her know he could hear everything being said.

She made a show of looking over the schedule again. "Maybe you should assign Jace to someone else. Team me with Saul. Or even Carnell." She swallowed her grimace at both offers. She didn't want to be assigned to either of them. It would limit her effectiveness at the summit.

"No. Carnell will be tactical command and computers only. He's not ready for active missions. Saul is better, but he's still not top-tier. Unless I see something over the next few days that makes me think Eakin doesn't have the skills I think he has, you two will be the Alpha team."

Everybody was important on a mission like protecting the LESS Summit, but the Alpha team was second in command to Derek, able to make judgment calls and decisions without approval when needed.

"Is that going to be a problem?" Derek asked when Lillian didn't respond. "There's obviously history between you two."

Yes, there was history, but she wasn't going to let that stop her from being as effective as possible. From making the entire team be as effective as possible. They'd need to be as strong as they could for whatever Damien Freihof had planned. Putting ancient history aside would be no problem.

Lillian glanced at Jace again, his blue eyes now piercing hers. She didn't look away. "No—no problem," she told Derek. "Our past was a long time ago. It's over. It was over before it even started."

It was over before it even started.

Lillian's quiet words stung even hours later. They shouldn't; after all, they were only the truth. Their relationship—at least the sexual side of it—had ended almost as soon as it began.

Trying to stick to the letting-bygones-be-bygones promise he made yesterday was proving a little more difficult than he had expected.

Jace pushed the entire conversation from his mind. There was no room for worrying about the distant past out here on the Gauntlet, which was a glorified obstacle course full of real-life dangers—fire, barbed wire and paintball-type ammunition that wouldn't seriously wound someone, but would hurt like hell if you got hit.

Harsh words were the least of his problems right now.

Evidently there was some sort of multimillion-dollar training simulator nearby, but the way everyone had started crossing themselves and balking when it was mentioned made him think it wasn't very popular.

So here they were, out in a wooded area, having just crawled 500 yards under barbed wire. He and Lillian were a team, moving together. There were four other two-person teams made up of the various SWAT members he'd met yesterday. This exercise was part race, part team-building.

It wasn't unlike some of the obstacles and exercises he'd been a part of as an Army Ranger. He understood the importance of pushing the body and the mind, and doing it with the person who was going to have your back when you went into battle. It looked like he and Lillian would be that person for each other.

And she wasn't too happy about it.

Unhappy because she was being forced to work with an ex? Or unhappy because that ex was a new person on the team who might recognize some suspicious behavior on her part that her other colleagues could miss?

Either way, she was pushing those feelings aside now. She seemed vaguely surprised that he was able to keep up with her rapid crab-crawl pace under the barbed wire, roughly eighteen inches over the ground. Her small stature gave her a decided advantage for an obstacle of this type, and Lily knew how to use it.

But Jace knew how to make his body move quickly also. Even though the wire was sometimes only an inch or two over his shoulders and back, he used his abdominal muscles to keep himself straight and low, speed from his long reach making up for the caution he had to use because of his size.

As they reached the last of the wire and rolled out, they took cover behind some trees.

"You're fast," she said.

"Not my first rodeo."

The rest of the teams were making their way along the ground, Philip Carnell having the most difficult time.

"Do we need to go back in and help Carnell?" he said.

Lillian gave a brief shake of her head. "No. Normally Derek doesn't even allow him to do this sort of training even though Carnell insists he should be given the chance. But he may be needed to do something besides provide tactical assistance next week in Denver, so today he's in."

"Is he going to make it?" Carnell's partner was Saul Poniard, who might also be new, but was light-years ahead of Carnell when it came to physical abilities.

"Saul will get him through hopefully. And we'll get Philip out as a team if he needs it.

Not that he'll thank us for it." Lillian shook her head. "As Alpha team, we're going to have our own problems. We'll need to take out the sniper before he picks everyone off."

"Sniper?"

Lillian grinned. "You didn't think Derek was going to miss the fun, did you? That man loves his paintball gun. You and I will have to take him out before everyone else gets there. That's Alpha team's primary challenge."

"Then let's get moving."

They navigated a series of obstacles, including a fifty-foot rope climb, before coming to a pile of five large, heavy logs.

"Each of these has to be maneuvered through this next section." Lillian referred to the logs. "Every two-person team is responsible for one log. We choose to make it either hard on us or hard on the other teams coming behind us."

Jace raised an eyebrow. "So…heaviest?"

Lillian's smile was huge and he had to fight to keep it from taking his breath away. "I was hoping you'd agree. But it's not going to be easy."

"Then I guess you better stop grinning like an idiot and get to it."

Jace couldn't stop the grin on his own face, either. Lily wanted to push herself. That was something he understood. He had known it about her even back in the day, and it was one of the reasons he had thought the army would be such a good fit for her also.

He tamped down the spring of bitterness over the way things had turned out. Bygones. Much more important to focus on the problems at hand.

The log was damn heavy. The exercise required them to lift the log over some obstacles, under others, and even carry it over their heads as they crossed a small creek.

Lillian never complained, never slipped in supporting her part of the awkward piece of wood. By the time they threw it down half a mile later, they were both pushing the edges of exhaustion. They slumped together against the back of a tree, shoulder to shoulder, so they could each catch their breath.

"Now we have to take out Derek and his evil paintball gun." Her eyes were closed as she allowed her body to attempt to recapture some of its strength just as he did.

"How do we do that with no gun of our own?"

"Technically for this exercise, all we have to do to defeat him is for one of us to make it over the finish line without getting hit." She didn't sound very enthused about the idea.

"Easier said than done?"

Those brown eyes opened. "Derek is a mastermind at this. Plus, he knows all our strengths. We have about a five-percent success rate when it comes to getting past him."

"What about splitting up and running from two different directions?"

She shook her head. "We've tried. It's such a narrow strip of land, he can cover it and almost always get both people before they get across. We don't have very much cover."

"What are the rules about just one person getting across? If that's all we need, we should wait for everyone else, protect one person and everyone else can take the hits."

"First, the hits aren't gentle. They hurt like hell." She obviously had firsthand knowledge. "Second, to keep us from always grouping, the rule is, whoever makes it across the finish line unhit has two minutes to get the wounded the fifteen yards across no-man's-land. Almost impossible if it's one person trying to get multiple people across. And particularly impossible with the group coming up behind us."

Jace leaned his head back against the tree. He could hear the frustration in her voice. The Omega SWAT team was not up to the level it usually was. Too many new people. Too many wounded.

"I have a plan," he said.

Now he had her full attention.

"We'll use Derek's assumptions against him, with a little bit of trickery thrown in. But I'll warn you, this won't be easy. Particularly on you. We won't be playing to your strengths. But we will be using your strength."

She sat up. "Okay. I'm game. What's your plan?"

"Derek expects you and me to make a break before the rest of the team gets here. To try to overcompensate for their limitations. To use your speed and my strength to get everyone else through."

"And we're not going to do that?"

Jace just smiled.

Ten minutes later the other members of the team began catching up with them. Jace explained his plan. Everyone stared at Lillian once Jace told them what she would need to do.

Even Lillian looked a little skeptical.

"You can do it," he said.

"You're going to take a lot of hits," she responded. "Derek won't like it and won't show any mercy."

Jace grinned. "I can handle a few bruises."

"Are you sure you don't want me to make a dash for it?" Saul asked, enthusiasm fairly radiating from him. "I'm fast."

Jace shook his head. "No, that's exactly what

he's expecting. For you or Lily to run, to try to use your speed. And you're too big for me to use in this plan."

Saul grimaced. "Are you sure she can handle her end of this?"

Jace shook his head at the same time Lillian's eyes narrowed. Saul might be new, but he would learn fast not to underestimate Lillian if he wanted to stay part of this team. "Don't worry. I'll do my part."

It was a pretty damn big part.

Jace turned to Philip. "You've got to sell it, to get us more time. Derek will come after you just to teach you a lesson."

Philip didn't look thrilled, but then again, Jace wasn't sure he ever did.

"I can handle a few bruises," Philip echoed.

Jace nodded at the other team members. They weren't excited about being left out of most of the action, but they understood the advantage of his plan. Of keeping Derek off balance as long as possible.

"Remember." Lillian turned to him. "Rules are that you can only take five more steps after you're hit. Make them count."

They all stood and made their way closer to the twenty-yard square area Derek was guarding. There was some cover of trees and boulders, but not a lot. Derek definitely had the tactical advantage.

Jace and Lillian separated from the rest of the team. Philip and Saul would be drawing Derek's attention—hopefully—from the other end of the field.

"If Saul gets all gung-ho and takes off, then gets hit, this isn't going to work," Lillian whispered. "I'm not sure it's going to work even if he doesn't."

Jace couldn't help himself—he bent down and kissed her, fast and hard. "If there's anyone I would trust to get me out of a situation when I'm wounded, it's you."

"You're nuts, Eakin." She shook her head. "Let's try this crazy plan."

They waited for the signal. It came just moments later.

"Because we have to stick together, Poniard, don't you dare leave me here to get shot." Philip's words were soft, like they weren't meant to be heard. Jace and Lillian could barely make them out.

But that meant Derek could, too.

Jace didn't wait. He scooped up Lillian—she rolled herself into as tight a ball as possible—and he ran. He only had to make it halfway before he got shot. Far enough that his back would be to Derek, and the team leader wouldn't see the hidden person Jace had curled in his arms. Derek would be expecting Lily to try to run her own route and make it through. Wouldn't expect her to agree to be carried.

"Damn it, Saul, wait!" Philip again, hopefully going from the script, and not saying it because Saul really had taken off.

It bought Jace the few extra seconds he needed. He kept Lillian tucked high against his chest as he felt the first paintball hit his back. Three more followed rapidly.

Damn, those *did* hurt.

This whole plan was relying on the fact that Derek wouldn't stay and watch Jace "fall" onto the boulder in front of him. He had too much else he had to keep track of. Jace got his five more steps in, then set Lillian on the ground. She immediately began sprinting toward the finish line.

Whooshes of air blew as more shots were fired from the paintball gun. But not at Lillian.

Philip squeaked, "Ow, damn it." He took his five steps closer to the finish line, then fell.

Jace turned to watch and saw the exact moment Derek realized he'd been played. He turned and aimed his gun at Lillian, but she was already crossing the line.

Derek smiled and looked down at his watch.

"Okay, Muir. You've got two minutes to get them both across if you want to claim your victory."

Lillian sprinted back to Philip first. She sat him up and then swung his arm over her shoulder, dragging him across to the safe area.

She stopped to take a breath, looking Jace in the eye. He weighed significantly more than Philip did.

But Jace had no doubt she could do it—that she would get him over to that safe zone. Especially now, with the entire team looking on.

She jogged back to him and got down to business. The boulder helped, putting Jace more upright. But she would still have to fireman-carry him. There was no way she could drag him like she had done with Philip.

He could hear the cheers of their teammates as she pulled his torso around her shoulders and slipped her hand through his legs and wrapped her arm around his knees. A huge groan came out of her small body as her legs straightened and she took his whole weight, lifting him off the ground.

She couldn't walk straight, and she might not have been able to walk for long—especially after the grueling workout they'd already gone through on the course—but Lillian got them both over the finish line just as the time was running out.

Jace immediately dropped his leg to the ground and took his weight as the rest of the team ran over, hooting and hollering. Even Philip was grinning. Lillian dropped back against a tree to get her breath. Everyone was slapping both of them on the back until Derek came over and told them to complete the rest of the course.

"Good job, you two," he told them as they walked to the next section. "Completely had me fooled. Some partnerships are just meant to be."

Jace didn't say anything. He'd once thought that exact same thing also.

He'd been wrong.

Chapter Six

Everything seemed to take a turn for the better after the Gauntlet in terms of team building. The paintball win had given them all the boost they'd needed and the confidence that they could work together successfully. Lillian was glad to see it.

What she wasn't quite so glad about was that Jace seemed to be within arm's reach every time she turned around for the next five days.

All the damn time.

Admittedly, a lot of it was the training they were doing as a team. More obstacle courses. The shooting range. The different scenarios within the multimillion-dollar simulator on the outskirts of the Omega Sector campus.

It came as no surprise to her that Jace fit right into the team as if he'd been there all along. He'd always been charming and affable even back when they were teenagers. The polar opposite of his bastard brother. Tension coursed through her body at the thought of Daryl, so Lillian pushed him from her mind. She'd had twelve years of practice doing that.

But charm meant nothing to a SWAT team without the skills to back it up. Jace had those in spades, too, and they'd been especially evident when he'd proven himself with the Gauntlet plan. His sharpshooting abilities impressed even Ashton Fitzgerald, the team's sharpshooter. Jace's close-quarters fighting skills she already personally knew about. He also had a specialty in explosive devices.

When Ashton, team clown, asked Jace if he would go steady with him, Lillian knew Jace had won over the team.

Saul and Philip weren't too happy about Jace's instant inclusion into the inner circle, when they'd both been fighting so hard for that same acceptance. But there was just an innate authority with Jace that neither Saul nor Philip had. Nobody said anything about it, but they all knew it.

The parts of Jace that had drawn her when they were both teenagers were even more prevalent now. His strength. His focus. His dedication.

Add that to the fact that he was opening a ranch where he would raise animals that would help soldiers with PTSD? How was she supposed to process that?

She wanted distance from him but couldn't get it. There literally was no time. The LESS Summit was coming up in just days and they would all need to function seamlessly as a team by then.

They trained day and night, since the summit would require them in both daylight and nighttime hours. Sometimes that meant little sleep or crashing on whatever couch or floor was available in the team break room.

Jace definitely wasn't a diva. Just like everyone else, when they had a break in the middle of a twenty-four-hour training session, he found a spot, curled his head back and promptly fell asleep.

But damn it, that had ended up being right next to her every single time.

Just like how every time they were at the practice range he ended up next to her.

And every time they were in the SWAT van traveling somewhere, it was his leg pressed up against hers.

When they ate. When they did their ten-mile runs.

Always there. Always next to her.

He never did anything to make any sort of

big deal out of it, hadn't kissed her again or made any moves on her since that brief kiss at the Gauntlet. But he didn't have to. Lillian was aware of him in a way she hadn't been aware of someone…for twelve years.

And it felt good. In the scariest way possible.

Her body and mind trusted Jace in a way she hadn't been able to trust another man in twelve years…actually her whole life. She wasn't well versed in psychology—damn, she missed Grace Parker—but Lillian knew enough about her own mind to know that the passion between the two of them a dozen years ago was the only untainted memory of sex that she had.

Sometimes she still thought about those nights they'd had together. How uninhibited and all-encompassing her feelings had been. They'd had the entire world and forever in their future. No grasp at all of how quickly life could change.

She and Jace had been friends for a long time before they were lovers, since Jace was older than her and refused to sleep with her until she turned eighteen. Then they'd only had about a month after her eighteenth birthday before…

Before he left for the army. Before everything in her world crumbled. Lillian felt her body turn cold even now.

Jace seemed to have forgiven her for *leaving* him—God, the thought still made her want to vomit—for Daryl.

It was good that he'd forgiven her, without even having one iota of understanding about the true circumstances.

Jace was a good man. He'd been a good man then, and he was still a good man now. So she was glad he had gotten over his sense of betrayal at her perceived actions.

And if she had any choice in the matter, Jace would go to his grave being the man who was good enough to forgive an ex-girlfriend for running off with his brother. He would never know the truth.

Because that would just hurt him so much worse.

"What are you thinking about over there?" Jace's voice broke in to her thoughts. "Whatever it is, it can't be good."

This time he was across the table from her in the Omega canteen. It was lunchtime, and while they had been here all night for a dark-based training op, they'd all be leaving to go home for a break soon. The team would be going to Denver tomorrow.

She shrugged, ignoring his question, since there was no way in hell she was going to answer it truthfully anyway.

"You worried about something concerning the summit?" he asked between bites of his sandwich.

This she could answer. "To be honest, I'm concerned about everything to do with this summit. Hitting something this high-profile may not align perfectly with Damien Freihof's MO, but I think it aligns with his mind-set."

"I thought Freihof had been using other people to do his dirty work. Stirring up the pot with people in the past who had an ax to grind with Omega agents and helping him try to get their revenge."

"He has." Lillian's hands balled into fists. "But then he killed Grace Parker, our team psychiatrist, himself. Brutally, and in front of everyone. I think he's escalating. And I think trying to humiliate Omega by attacking the summit would definitely suit his purposes."

"Sounds like he has it in for you guys. What's that about?"

"Evidently we had a hand in his wife's death. She was killed when Omega went in on a bank raid."

"Freihof brought his wife along when he robbed a bank?"

"No. Freihof has been involved with a lot of different criminal activities for the last fifteen years. But in this case, evidently they both just happened to be in the wrong place at the wrong time. Someone was robbing the bank, the wife freaked out and tried to make a run for it when SWAT arrived, and she got shot and killed. By us. And Freihof has decided to make everyone who has ever been a part of Omega Sector pay for that mistake."

Jace seemed to process all that as he ate. "And he maybe has someone helping him? Someone inside Omega?"

Lillian shrugged. "There's been no official word, but a lot of rumors. And some of the stuff Freihof has known, he couldn't possibly have known without help from the inside. I have no doubt there's a traitor within Omega, as much as I hate to say it. But like Derek said, we can't all go around accusing one another of being the mole and expect to work effectively as a team."

Jace nodded, studying her.

It had been a long few days and they were all supposed to go home and rest. They would all need to be on high alert at the summit.

If Lillian was Freihof, the summit was where she would strike. If he could take down the LESS device, he would be serving a great blow to law enforcement all over the country. Doing that while humiliating Omega Sector seemed to be cut directly out of his playbook.

Not to mention the summit would be crowded with politicians, law-enforcement leaders and ordinary people there to observe or protest. Plenty of people to try to hurt or kill.

"You headed out?" Jace asked as they finished up their food.

She wasn't particularly interested in going back to her empty apartment. She tended to spend as little time there as possible. But no need to advertise that fact. "Absolutely. We all need to get a little R and R before heading to Denver."

The rest of the team had already left. Most of the guys had families now. A lot of times Lillian was invited over to their houses for meals or just to hang out. But not right now. The wound of losing Grace Parker was still too fresh, too open. All the guys just wanted to be with their wives and children and hold them close and thank God for them.

Lillian wasn't going to boo-hoo just because there was nobody thanking God she was alive. If Jace wasn't here, she would probably head out to a bar and find a guy to hook up with for a few hours. It was never fulfilling, and sometimes it was downright scary the way she checked out emotionally during sex, the way she didn't remember any of it even though it had happened just a few minutes before.

But anything was better than sitting at home alone.

Yet something about Jace being nearby made the thought of some random, emotionless hookup seem even more unappealing.

"How about you?" she asked him. "I don't even know where you're staying."

"Hotel a few blocks from here. There didn't seem to be much point in renting a place, since I was only going to be here a couple weeks. And I didn't want to have to drive back and forth every day from my ranch."

That made sense. And they were probably paying him enough to make it worth his while anyway.

"Okay." She nodded. "I guess I'll see you tomorrow."

"Yeah, see you tomorrow."

They dumped their trays and headed off in separate directions for the men's and women's locker rooms.

Lillian was used to being in here by herself. It usually didn't bother her. As a matter of fact, there had been plenty of times when she had to change clothes in front of the guys. She honestly didn't even think they saw her as a woman anymore.

She hardly saw *herself* as a woman anymore. She had all the woman parts but didn't tend to have many of the emotions that were tied to the female gender. She couldn't remember the last time she had cried.

She didn't mind being the only female on the team. She respected her colleagues, they respected her and they trusted her to do her job. She would die before she let down the team. She was part of something bigger and more important than herself, and she loved that.

But right now she just felt pretty damn alone. Not to mention all ramped up to get to the action tomorrow.

So she might as well stay here for a while longer and look over again the plans of the Denver city hall, officially known as the Denver City and County Building, where the summit would take place.

The LESS device was something that would change the face of law enforcement forever. Would allow a true merging of technology in all branches. The ramifications would be significant. Interstate cooperation would be much easier with the LESS system.

It was her job—the team's job—to make sure that happened. Studying the building plans one more time could only help.

She brought her duffel bag out of the changing room with her and moved to the main computer work space area in their building. SWAT members didn't have their own desks, but they had computers available for the team's use. They were mostly used for training, updating education, or situations like this, where someone wanted more details about the particulars of an op.

The big desk gave her plenty of room to set up a notebook and take some notes, as she brought up the building plans.

The 3-D replication of the building allowed her to take a virtual tour. Extremely helpful. But she knew that whatever she could find on a computer, Damien Freihof could, too.

She studied the plans for nearly an hour, going over each window, doorway, elevator shaft and staircase. She wanted to be able to find her way around the building even if she was blindfolded.

She closed down her browser and drew the plans of the first floor from memory, then compared it back to the actual drawing. Pretty close.

Lillian sat back in her chair, stretching her arms over her head and her legs out in front of her. That was enough for today. She'd already been up all night with the training. It was time to go home.

She just wished she had someone to go home to.

She shut down the computer and stood up, giving a small gasp when she saw Jace leaning against the wall a few feet behind her.

"You're lucky I didn't have a weapon, Eakin. What the hell are you doing standing there all stalker-like?"

"I didn't want to interrupt your memorization exercise."

"I wanted to make sure I was as familiar with the building as I could be. I thought you had already left."

"Smart. And no, not yet. I had a little bit of work to do here."

She couldn't help noticing how good he looked in jeans and a black long-sleeved shirt rolled up at the wrists. He even had his boots on. He'd owned similar ones back in the day.

His brown hair was cut shorter than it had been then, closer to military regulation, although it had obviously grown out a little bit. The tips of her fingers itched with the need to run her hands through it. Those icy blue eyes stared at her with a touch of friendliness and something she couldn't quite discern.

But one thing she could discern for certain: he was the sexiest-looking thing she had seen in a long time. Whatever she was feeling right now definitely wasn't emotionless. The opposite, in fact.

There would never be anything emotionless when it came to her and Jace Eakin.

The thought of feeling something—something *real*—while a man touched her had Lillian crossing to Jace. Just once she wished she was more of a high-heels-and-short-skirt sort of girl. A girl who knew how to do something with her hair besides pull it back in a ponytail. A girl who knew how to put on makeup to cause her eyes to look mysterious and sultry.

A girl who knew how to seduce a man like Jace.

But she wasn't that girl. All she could do was make her offer straight up with no pretense.

She stopped when she was directly in front of him. From this close, all she could do was remember that kiss from a few days ago in the parking lot.

"If you're done with your work, why don't you come over to my apartment? We've got eighteen hours before we have to report back here. Seems like we ought to be able to find something to do with that time."

Passion—the same heat she felt—flared in his eyes for just a moment as he eased closer to her. She felt his fingers grip her hips and knew she would feel those lips on hers again any second. There was nothing she wanted more in the world. Those kisses, as much as she'd tried to tamp them down, had never been far from her conscious mind.

But then his fingers clenched on her body for just a second before letting her go. He stepped back. Her eyes flew up to his, but his handsome face was carefully masked.

"I don't think that's such a good idea. For a number of reasons."

Everything that had been burning inside Lillian turned to ice. She took a step back, feeling like he'd slapped her.

"Tiger Lily, it's not that I don't feel the attraction," he continued.

Maybe she'd been wrong, maybe he hadn't truly been able to forgive her for leaving him. "It's about before. About Daryl. Right?"

He shook his head. "No. It's not even that. It's about now, and us being a team and…"

She waited for him to finish, but he didn't. Whatever he *wasn't* saying was just as important as what he was. But ultimately it came down to one thing, didn't it?

She took another short step back from him. "And we really don't know each other, do we? Not anymore." Something flickered in his eyes and he reached for her again, but Lillian moved smoothly out of his reach. "You're right, Jace, this is probably a bad idea. The team has to come first. And casual hookups probably just aren't your thing."

His dark head tilted to the side. "Are they yours? They weren't at one time."

She knew he was talking about how she had felt about her mother when Lillian was growing up. How she'd disdained her mother's constant revolving door of men. How she swore she would never be that way. That sex would never be a meaningless act.

She laughed softly even as she felt the wounded heart she hid deep inside crack a little further. For a long time, Lillian hadn't thought about that promise she'd made to herself. How she'd utterly broken it. She couldn't even blame it on Daryl. That had been all on her. "I guess we all change. Grow up. Face the real world."

"Lily..."

Lillian knew she had to get out of here. She couldn't continue to face his blue eyes without crumbling. Knew that if he asked her about her secrets now she would tell him.

She closed her eyes and regrouped. When she opened them a couple seconds later, she was able to put a smirk on her face. She punched Jace good-naturedly on the arm. "Get some rest, Eakin. I'll catch you tomorrow. Big day."

Without another word she turned, grabbed her bag and walked out the door.

Alone. As always.

Chapter Seven

The next morning when the team met at Omega Sector headquarters in preparation to depart to the LESS Summit, Jace wanted to punch a wall.

Still wanted to punch a wall. He'd wanted to do so ever since yesterday afternoon, when Lillian offered…whatever it was she had offered.

He hadn't known how to handle it. On one hand, there was nothing he wanted more than to get Lillian in his bed. His body didn't seem to care what had happened between them twelve years ago, or care that she might be the traitor.

But he found that he couldn't betray her in that way. Couldn't take her to bed just to get close to her to find out more about her activities. Ridiculous that he would take her feelings into consideration when it came to the issue of betrayal.

He'd watched her yesterday on the computer for a long time. She'd been so focused she hadn't even realized he was there. She'd studied the building plans, examining them over and over until she was able to draw them without looking.

Unfortunately, the action didn't necessarily prove her innocence. Maybe she was studying the plans because she wanted to be as prepared as she could possibly be as a member of the SWAT team.

Or maybe she was studying the building plans because she had nefarious reasons of her own.

All Jace could say for sure was that she had not tried to communicate with anyone or leave any sort of cryptic messages while he'd been watching, as the mole had been known to do.

Jace's gut said the same thing about her now that it had said about her back in Ren's office: she was not the traitor. But God knew his gut had been wrong about Lillian before.

He'd basically glued himself to her side for the past week and all he'd found was that she was a damn fine SWAT team member. He hadn't found anything else that would suggest she was the mole. Lillian had secrets, Jace had no doubt whatsoever that she had secrets. But he didn't think those secrets had anything to do with national security.

That look on her face when she'd mentioned casual sex was still haunting him. Hell, Jace hadn't been a saint for the last decade. He'd had plenty of casual relationships with women in that time. He didn't hold a double standard. If Lillian had chosen to have a slew of casual sexual encounters, that was her prerogative.

What gutted him had been the look in her eyes, the completely humorless laugh, when she said that those sexual encounters had been her choice. Obviously somewhere deep inside she wasn't okay with it. She was hurting herself.

Steve Drackett's words of concern about possible sexual assault in her past had been echoing in Jace's mind for the last eighteen hours. Ever since Lillian had offered a casual hookup with eyes that told him she hated herself.

He was back to wanting to punch a wall again.

Not to mention he'd turned her down, which had probably stung also, even though he was doing it—or *not* doing it—for the right reasons.

Regardless, Lillian was now in a different vehicle on the way to Denver this morning. She'd been coldly polite to him as they'd all worked together to pack up equipment. Not unfriendly or rude, just obviously not interested in prolonging any conversations with him. The closeness they'd been building through sheer proximity over the last week was now completely gone.

Jace had no doubt Lillian would be coolly professional to him throughout the mission. That wasn't going to help him get close enough to her to find out if she was the one sabotaging Omega Sector. But he wasn't going to sleep with her to get that info, either.

Especially not after how she had looked at him yesterday, with such shadows in those brown eyes.

Jace was going to have to concentrate on the mission in front of him. At this point, if the mole was going to strike, and Lillian was that mole, all he could do was be close enough to stop it. After that, hell if he knew what he would do if she was the mole.

The LESS Summit started in two days. Already people were gathering in Denver. It was going to be crowded, full of angry and excited people. The situation was already hectic; throw in a potential terrorist attack and the situation became even worse.

They didn't even make it all the way into downtown Denver before they hit trouble.

"Change in plans, everybody," Derek said from the front seat as the SUV picked up speed. "Just got a call from Denver PD. Evidently, as expected, all the crazies have rolled into town with word of the LESS Summit. There's a jumper on a highway bridge and we're closest. They need our help."

Jace could see the shift come over the team, especially the more experienced ones.

"A jumper? As in someone trying to commit suicide?" Philip asked. "Why the hell is SWAT being called in? Just let the person jump."

Nobody responded. Being part of a SWAT team was not just about hunting bad guys, shooting and securing buildings. Sometimes it was about defusing situations. Helping people who didn't know how to help themselves. It had been the same for the US Army Rangers.

If someone couldn't understand that, they probably shouldn't be on the team at all. This was probably a big part of the reason Carnell was only temporary.

"Shut up, Philip," Saul muttered, rolling his eyes. Everyone else was obviously thinking the same thing.

They pulled up at the bridge crossing the highway. Local police were stopping traffic on either side of the road, where a man was standing on the highest part of the overpass, on the outside of the railing, one arm around a light post.

If he let go, there would be nothing to stop him from flying onto the busy highway below.

As they got out of the vehicle, a uniformed

officer came running over to them. Derek showed him credentials and the officer fully admitted to being in over his head.

"He's been out there for about ten minutes. Hasn't said a word."

Lillian and the rest of the team from the second vehicle jogged over to where they were.

"Okay." Derek glanced at the man's chest to get his name. "Officer Milburn, we're going to take over if that's all right with you."

Milburn nodded enthusiastically.

"Everybody on open comms, channel A," Derek continued. "Ashton, Saul, Jace—you need to clear everyone else off this bridge. Everybody wants to be a YouTube sensation, but let's not make it easy. Carnell, get on the laptop. As soon as we can get this guy's name, you find whatever info you can on him. Lillian, you're with me."

Lillian shook her head. "Derek, you know I'm no good with the touchy-feely stuff."

Derek nodded. "Just in case he responds to a woman better than a man. Lillian and I will be on open comms. None of us deal with this sort of situation a lot, so if you've got insight, let us have it."

The open comm channel meant that everyone could hear anytime someone else spoke without them having to press a button. It could be chaotic, but in a situation like this, also useful. Jace jogged over to the other side of the bridge and moved the barrier back farther. They couldn't stop people from recording what was happening, but like Derek had said, they could make it as difficult as possible.

Jace heard Derek ask the man his name. Ask if it was okay if they stood there and talked. Explained that they wouldn't come near him.

Derek did everything right. But the man wasn't interested in talking.

"Hey, guys." It was Saul. "I've got an empty vehicle over here that doesn't belong to anyone. Registration of the vehicle says it belongs to an Oliver Lewis."

"Start running the name, Philip," Derek said softly. "You try talking to him, Lillian."

Jace watched as Lillian took her turn, easing a little closer to the man. "Hi, sir, my name is Agent… Lillian. My name is Lillian. Can you just tell us your name?"

The man shook his head.

"Is your name Oliver Lewis?" Lillian continued gently. "There's a car registered to someone named Oliver Lewis. Is that you?"

"Don't come any closer," the man said even though they hadn't moved. "You can't stop me."

"No, sir," Derek said immediately, hands out.

"We won't come any closer. We just want to know if that's your name."

The man gave the tiniest of nods.

"That was a confirmation on the ID," Jace said so Derek wouldn't have to take a chance on talking and spooking the guy. "Run everything you have on him, Carnell. Hurry."

Derek and Lillian continued to try to get Oliver to talk, but without much success. Finally Philip came back on the comm.

"Oliver Lewis. Twenty-seven years old. Married. Got out of the army six months ago after nine years in."

Lillian turned away from Oliver to look over at him. "Jace, you try."

He met her eyes from across the bridge, but spoke softly into the comm unit. "I don't have any background in this sort of thing."

"But you're military. Maybe he'll respond to you."

"Yes, Jace," Derek whispered. "We're not getting through to him at all. If anything we're doing more harm."

He could at least try. He jogged up, slowing to a walk as he neared.

"Oliver," Derek said, "this is Jace Eakin. Jace isn't a normal part of our team, he just stepped in to help out."

"Yeah," Jace agreed. "I just got out of the

service. They needed some help here with all the protests and stuff happening in Denver this week, so I'm assisting."

"You were in the service?"

"Army. Tenth Special Forces group."

"Ranger," Oliver whispered, turning to look at Jace for the first time.

Lillian and Derek were backing away to give Jace and Oliver some semblance of privacy. Jace nodded. "That's right. You army also?"

"How did you know that?"

"Not many people would know that the Tenth Special Forces group are Rangers unless they'd been in the army themselves. How long have you been out?"

"Six months."

Jace took the slightest step closer. "How long were you in?"

"Since I was eighteen. Was the only thing I've ever known. And now…" He trailed off.

Jace nodded. "Adjusting back to civilian life can be really difficult. Especially if you did some hard tours."

"Two back-to-back in Afghanistan."

Jace asked Oliver questions about his tours. Where he'd been located. Tried to get him to talk about friends, other men and women who'd served in his unit. He continually shifted closer under the guise of discussion, or leaned against the railing, or just listened.

Although it really wasn't a guise at all.

Jace would've sat and listened for however long Oliver wanted. People like him were the reason he was opening his ranch in Colorado. For guys like Oliver, who just needed somewhere to go for a while as they sorted out the mess in their head, tried to adjust back into a world that didn't always fit how they'd been trained.

"Oliver," Jace finally said after they'd talked for nearly twenty minutes. "Why don't you step back over the railing? Whatever it is you're feeling? Let's just wait it out, try to find another way. A less permanent solution to whatever's going on with you."

"I hit my wife," Oliver responded, his tone dripping with remorse. "I freaked out during a nap and punched her in the face. She's pregnant, Jace. How can I be trusted to be around her? To be around a baby, for God's sake. I'm toxic."

Jace tensed, prepared to make a dive for Oliver if he let go of the railing right now. He was almost close enough to pull back.

"We've already got the wife on the way, Jace." Derek's voice came through the comm.

"She's been frantic looking for him. Definitely doesn't want him to do this."

"That's really hard, man." Jace might not be schooled in talking down a potential suicide victim, but he knew enough not to discount Oliver's feelings. "Have you talked to her since it happened?"

"Why would she ever want to talk to me again?"

"How long have you two been married?"

Oliver glanced at him. "Four years."

"Well, maybe your wife doesn't want to throw out four years' worth of good, just because of one moment of bad."

"She woke me up in the middle of a nightmare and I hit her. Hard. Before I even knew what was happening. Could've broken her jaw. She was scared of me. I could see it."

Jace nodded. "Yeah, but knowing she might have to give you space and wanting you to end your life are two different things. You can see that, right?"

Oliver shrugged. But at least he was holding on to the railing again.

"Listen," Jace continued, "I know this isn't an answer to all your problems, and you and your wife are going to need to work through a lot, it sounds like. But I have a ranch I'm setting up, just outside Colorado Springs. Horses, dogs, hell, even a few cats. It's a place for vets to come, spend some time."

"You're just making that up. Just trying to get me to come down."

"No, man, I'm not. Like Derek said, I'm just helping out with law enforcement temporarily. The ranch is going to be my full-time work. Soldiers can come, sort stuff out in their head while riding or walking or just hanging out with the animals. People like you, Oliver. Because if you feel this bad about what happened with your wife, that means you want to do what's right. I can't guarantee the ranch will help, but it's at least worth a try before you leave your unborn child with no father at all."

"You're not lying?" For the first time, there was the slightest bit of hope in Oliver's voice. "This place really exists?"

"I give you my word, as one man who served to another, I am not lying. You can be the first person to come visit. Hell, you can come help me get everything set up."

Oliver just stared at him.

"This bridge is always going to be here, Oliver." Jace knew this might not be the right thing to say, but it was the truth. "There will always be a way to kill yourself if you want to go that route. But today why don't you choose to do something different? To give life a chance and see if there's any way to fix things that maybe a few months from now might not be as broken as you think."

Oliver stared at him for a long time before finally nodding and stepping one leg back on the safe side of the railing. As soon as his other leg was also over, Jace crossed the few feet to the man and pulled him in for a hug.

"I was telling the truth," Jace said. "I don't know what happens now, but I'll make sure you get the information about the ranch."

Jace stepped back when he heard a woman screaming Oliver's name and running toward him. She didn't give him any choice but to catch her as she leaped at him, sobbing.

The size of the bruise covering half her face left no doubt that this was Oliver's wife. But instead of being mad, she pulled back from him and cupped his cheeks in her hands. "Together. Whatever it is, we get through it *together*."

As he walked back to the rest of the team, Jace realized Oliver probably wasn't going to need his ranch. He was one of the lucky ones. Oliver had the support he needed right at home.

Chapter Eight

Lillian punched the lumpy pillow under her head as she lay in the too-soft hotel bed. Damn things were keeping her from getting any sleep.

Who was she kidding? The bed and pillow had nothing to do with her not getting rest. She never slept well outside her own bed. Hell, she didn't sleep all that great in her own.

Too much time, alone, in the dark, to think… to remember? Not her friend.

Daytime and her job at Omega Sector allowed her to stay busy, to stay focused, to push herself to her limits.

To keep the demons at bay.

But nighttime, especially after a day like today, when she hadn't expended a great deal of physical energy? Not as easy. The darkness seemed to press in on her.

How many times had she come back to her senses in a bed sort of like this one with a guy she didn't quite remember, her skin crawling with the knowledge of what she'd done? Again.

Jace had been right to turn her down. She was damaged in ways that would taint every relationship she had. And it might have started with Daryl, but Lillian couldn't deny that her own choices, the patterns she allowed to take over in her sexual escapades, were what had perpetuated the problem.

And watching Jace today, talking to that vet, connecting to the man on such an honest, authentic level... Lillian rubbed her chest in the general vicinity of her heart. He was going to raise dogs, horses. Animals that would help people who'd been traumatized by war.

She couldn't help wondering if a dog might help her through the trauma of a different kind of war. Maybe it could provide the companionship she'd refused to acknowledge she so desperately needed.

Who was she kidding? She couldn't take care of a puppy. A dog needed attention. Love. A regular schedule. She wasn't capable of any of those.

She glanced at her watch to find it was 3:30 a.m. and swung her legs around to the floor. She might as well get up. She knew well enough she wouldn't be able to get back to sleep.

Knew that it was just a matter of time before

the darkness around her—even though she had a light on in the bathroom—started to eat at her sanity. Lillian *never* slept in the dark

She would go for a walk. It was what she usually did. Although sometimes those walks led her to a local bar and then to the home of some nameless guy for meaningless sex. She always hoped that it might be different. That she might connect. *Feel* something.

She had no desire to go find some random guy now. The kisses with Jace had just reminded her how utterly empty those other encounters were. Attempts to punish herself, Grace had said. Lillian had scoffed. What did she have to punish herself for? she'd argued.

But Lillian knew the list was long and never far from her mind. And growing.

For not being able to fight back against Daryl.

For not being strong enough to escape and go to Jace.

For not having the guts to admit to him—then or now—what had happened and why she was so broken.

For not being able to stop Freihof from killing Grace and hurting others.

Lillian was dressed in her cargo pants and T-shirt in under a minute. She grabbed her jacket from the closet and left the voices behind.

The chill of the February air helped chase away the voices. There weren't many people around this area of downtown at this hour. The bars had already let out, and most of the buildings were government or offices anyway—no one was burning the midnight oil.

Lillian found herself wandering down toward the Denver City and County Building, the picturesque government building where the LESS Summit would be taking place.

The massive white marble building was iconic in the state of Colorado, beautiful and dignified. Although she knew the plans almost by heart, she wandered around it slowly, getting a feel for it from the outside. It would not be an easy building to secure. Multiple entrances and exit points in the form of doors and windows. The doors would need to be secure, although the windows had alarms and none of them would be open.

Lillian did a double take at one of the windows she was just thinking about on the far side of the building from where she stood.

Someone was easing themselves inside one of the windows lowest to the ground. The same windows that Omega, with the help of Denver PD, had secured earlier today after they'd finished with the attempted suicide.

Someone had missed a window. On purpose?

Was this Freihof entering the building now? The mole?

Silently, Lillian crouched down to grab her backup sidearm from its ankle holster in her boot and took off in a sprint toward the window. If this was Freihof, she was going to catch him and nail the son of a bitch.

Right. Damn. Now.

The window was still missing part of the grate that should've been covering it to stop this sort of entry into the building. Staying low, she gazed inside. The small basement storage room was dark and she couldn't see anyone. Whoever had entered had proceeded into the hallway.

Lillian holstered her weapon and edged herself through the window, thankful her size made it easier. Once inside, she crouched low again, weapon back in hand, looking and listening. She was fairly certain no one was in the room, but she didn't want to take a chance.

Once she knew the room was secure, she moved quickly to the door, opened it and glanced up and down the darkened hallway. This wasn't an area of the building used for daily government purposes. The hall was littered with unused desks and furniture, cleaning supplies and bookshelves.

Plenty of places for someone to hide. And

damn well too many areas where someone could leave an explosive device.

Lillian looked up and down the hall, trying to ascertain which way the suspect had run. This was a virtual maze of connected halls and doors. Was the perp trying to get up to the main section of the building?

She heard a muffled noise farther down one of the hallways and began to move toward it, stepping quickly but silently.

Now would be a good time for backup, but by the time they got here it would be too late. And the three-man private security force who patrolled this building at night wouldn't be much good against Freihof.

Lillian could still remember watching Freihof pull the knife across Grace Parker's throat, helpless to do anything to save her friend. If Freihof was in this building, Lillian wasn't going to lose him calling for backup. She'd take him down herself.

She eased farther down the hallway, coming to an intersecting one. She didn't know which way the perp had gone. She moved quickly down one hallway, only to find it came to a dead end at a locked door. Cursing, she spun around and ran back down to where the halls crossed, hoping the perp hadn't made it out.

She wished she'd studied this floor's plans as much as she had the other levels.

She took the corner too quickly and wasn't expecting the assailant to be right there. Mistake. She'd been too desperate to catch him to be as careful as she should have been.

She swallowed a cry as the perp hit her arms with a hardcover law book, knocking her gun to the floor and sending it skidding across the hall. Pain radiated through her right forearm at the force of the blow.

Mistake on his part, too. He should've clocked her with that book and knocked her out while he had the chance. He wouldn't get a second opportunity. Lillian spun back toward him, already perfectly balanced on her feet.

Her opponent was around six feet tall, probably close to two hundred pounds, and he was wearing a mask. Lillian was determined that would be coming off.

The guy dropped the book—smart, it would slow him down—and Lillian went on the offensive. She kicked him in the midsection, then used her momentum to swing her other leg around in a roundhouse kick to catch him in the head.

He blocked her kick at the last second, bringing his own fist around in a hook that would've knocked her to the floor, if not unconscious, if it had hit her jaw, where he was aiming.

Guy wasn't playing around.

Neither was she.

As always when fighting someone bigger and stronger, Lillian used her speed and agility to her advantage, keeping out of reach of his blows and using her legs and kicks as much as possible. The guy adapted quickly, bringing himself closer to her, so her legs couldn't inflict any damage. Also meant she had to stay focused in order to not get caught by one of his fists.

He had some skills.

She had more.

Lillian spun, her elbow connecting with the perp's jaw as she flung around. Momentum propelled him backward, allowing her to hit him with a right uppercut and then a left hook. He was going down and they both knew it.

Too late Lillian heard the click of a Taser and felt the voltage run through her body. Was there a second person here or had she just missed it?

She fought the blackness but it overcame her.

As soon as she came to, Lillian realized the direness of the situation.

A noose wrapped tightly around a neck had a very distinct feel.

She was sitting on a crate that rested precariously on a step in a stairwell. Her arms were tied behind her back. A few moments later the rope attached to her neck began to move upward as it was hoisted from the other side. Lillian could stand or she could suffocate.

The rope continued to move upward, pulling her up, until she was standing on the crate, then it kept going until she was on her very tiptoes.

The bands restraining her arms behind her back weren't that tight, but weren't so loose that she could get out.

"Someone has to take the fall," a voice whispered from the other side of the stairwell, near the door. Lillian couldn't tell whose it was. Someone she knew?

And that was why the restraints weren't tight on her arms. This needed to look like a suicide.

"This isn't going to work, you know. Whatever you have planned."

Lillian winced as the rope jerked the slightest bit higher as the masked man tied it to the door. The door pulled to the outside, which meant if someone opened it she was a goner.

So much for yelling for help.

She was on the very tops of her toes, the square crate balancing precariously on the rectangle step that was much more narrow.

"No one is going to believe I killed myself

with my arms tied behind my back." The words came out in breathy gasps as she focused on holding herself steady.

Masked Man just tilted his head, studying her. But she knew if he didn't cut her arms loose she had no chance of survival.

The box tipped forward and she felt sweat drip down her forehead as she attempted to get it back straight with what little leverage she had. She wasn't sure she had much chance for survival anyway.

The man moved away from the door and came up the stairs, giving her a wide berth—as if she could kick him and still maintain balance on the crate—and without another word cut the cord from her arms.

Lillian immediately brought her hands up above her head and took her weight from her legs, then swung her legs back down, twisting and using momentum to propel them toward Masked Man, hoping to catch him around the shoulders.

But he was expecting it and had moved up the stairs out of her reach. Her legs fell downward to the crate again, to give her arms supporting her weight a rest.

"Goodbye, Omega Sector."

She heard the whisper from behind her and saw an envelope drop to the floor before the crate was kicked out from under her. Immediately her arms took the weight of her body. She swung her legs up to try to wrap them around the rope, but couldn't, with the length and angle of the noose. She reached her foot out to the side, trying to reach the banister, and cursed when her legs weren't long enough to reach it.

She couldn't see the bastard behind her but knew he was waiting. Waiting to watch her die as her strength gave out and she couldn't support herself anymore.

She tried to yell—even if someone came rushing into the room, it wasn't going to do much more damage than her swaying here until her strength gave out—but the sound was cut off by the rope over her vocal chords. If she wanted to yell, she was going to have to use one hand to pull the rope away from the front of her throat. That meant supporting all her weight with one arm.

Her muscles were already straining from the constant state of pulling up. Supporting her weight with one arm wasn't going to work.

But she'd be damned if she was just going to die in front of this bastard.

She swung her legs up, trying to catch the upper part of the rope, but failed again. Even if she could get her legs hooked up there, she wasn't going to be able to get herself released.

She heard a low chuckle to her side. Bastard. He was enjoying this.

And then the alarm started blaring.

Masked Man muttered a curse and took off up the stairs. Lillian felt her arms begin to shake as the exhaustion from holding her own weight began to take its toll. If it wasn't for the rigorous SWAT training, she'd already be dead.

But even training wouldn't be enough. Physics would win. Her arms began to tremble more and she was forced to let go of the rope to give them a break.

Immediately the rope cut off all oxygen.

When everything began to go black, she reached up and grabbed the rope again. It wasn't long before the tremors took over.

She didn't want to go out like this. Wished she hadn't squandered this second chance she'd had with Jace in her life.

But even thinking of Jace, with his gorgeous blue eyes and cocky grin that still did things to her heart after all these years, couldn't give her any more strength.

She reached back up with her arms and found them collapsing before she even took her weight. Then the noose tightened and jerked around her neck, pulling her body forward, all air gone.

Blackness.

Chapter Nine

The door to the stairway was heavy as Jace opened it. Abnormally heavy, like someone was slumped against it. Fear coated his throat. Was it Lillian against the other side of the door, unconscious?

What he found when he pushed it open was much worse.

Jace immediately took in the situation, cursing violently as he flew up the steps toward Lillian's swinging form. "Lily!"

He dove to get himself under her legs and lift her, taking the weight off her throat and airway.

"Lillian? Lily? Come on, baby, talk to me."

His heart was a hammer in his chest as he wrapped his arms around her thighs and hoisted her up.

God, he couldn't be too late.

"Lily!" he yelled, shaking her and tapping her leg, trying to get her to wake up. The only thing he could hear was silence and the desperate beating of his own heart.

"Come on, Tiger Lily, damn it. Fight." Lillian Muir was nothing if not a fighter.

Jace reached into his pocket for his army knife, trying to position himself where he could hold her weight and saw through the rope above her head. He still couldn't tell if she was breathing or not.

Holding all her weight while on the awkward stairs made cutting the rope nearly impossible. But there was no way in hell he was going to let her go.

"Hand me the knife."

Lillian's hoarse whisper sent relief flooding through Jace. He gave her the knife, lifting her body farther to provide her the slack in the rope she needed. A minute later she fell completely into his arms as she finished cutting the binding around her throat.

He set them both on the stairs and pushed her clawing fingers away from the noose, loosening it and lifting it over her head. She slumped back against the wall.

There was already angry red marks and bruising on her neck and throat where the rope had been suffocating her.

"Jesus, Lily." Jace hauled her to him in a fierce

hug, swallowing the terror that still scratched at his insides. "What the hell happened?"

He was thankful when she didn't try to pull away. "Masked man." Her voice was painfully hoarse. "Saw someone crawl through a window and I followed him. He must've had a partner. Bastard Tasered me. When I woke up, he had me strung up, standing on a box. Then he tipped it."

"Damn it." Jace's eyes closed again. "You were holding your own weight up?"

She nodded and silence fell between them as Jace realized how close to death she'd really been. The fact that she was sitting here alive right now was a testament to both her physical and mental strength. Strength very few people had.

"Sick bastard. Why didn't he just shoot you?"

She pulled back from him and grabbed a note from behind him on the stairs. He unfolded it.

I CAN'T LIVE WITH WHAT I'VE DONE. WITH BETRAYING MY COLLEAGUES. SO MY FIGHT ENDS HERE.

It was written in block letters, which had been smart. It would've been difficult to prove whether Lillian had written it or not, which was exactly what the killer wanted.

"He wanted to make it look like a suicide," she whispered.

"We need to get you to a hospital and report to Derek. Let him know what's going on."

She pulled away from him, shaking her head. "I don't need a hospital. We go to Derek first. I'll get the team medic to check me out."

Jace grimaced but knew Lillian was probably right. There wasn't much a hospital could do for her except help her manage her pain. "Fine. But if your throat starts feeling any worse, you have to let someone know immediately. Swelling could still be an issue. And swelling could mean airway blockage."

She tilted her head, studying him. "How do you know that?"

"I had a little bit of medical training in the army."

She nodded and he could tell even that small movement caused her discomfort. "Okay, I'll tell you if it gets any worse."

"We need to let the building guards know about that window. It shouldn't have been missed in the security sweep."

He kept a hand at the small of her back as they moved through the door and toward the elevators.

"Maybe they weren't missed." Her voice was low, husky. "Maybe someone deliberately left it unsecured."

"You think the mole is here in Denver?"

"I think it's awfully suspicious that the guy who broke in was wearing a mask. He would've blended in better without it."

"A mask definitely screams *bad guy.*"

"Exactly. Why bother with it at all if nobody's going to recognize you anyway?"

Jace nodded as he led Lillian into the main lobby of the building. The guards were surprised to see them, and they had to show their identification quickly to keep the security team from calling backup.

Backup Lillian could've desperately used twenty minutes ago.

Without going into too much detail—particularly until they could talk to Derek and figure out a plan—Jace informed the guards about the unsecured window and that Lillian had followed someone in.

Lillian and Jace waited as the security team followed their protocol and brought in other members of the staff, as well as police. They showed them the window so it could be secured, and the area was swept for possible DNA. Whomever Lily had fought would be long gone by now, but maybe they would get lucky and get some sort of forensic clue to point them in the right direction.

Ultimately, there needed to be a great deal more security in this building, but not just the type that was barely paid more than minimum wage. City hall would need to be reswept. If Derek didn't make the decision to move the LESS Summit to the secondary location.

Jace kept an eye on Lillian as they left the building and walked back toward the hotel, carefully watching for signs that her throat was swelling and closing off. Although she moved stiffly—he couldn't even imagine what sort of trauma her upper body muscles had been through trying to hold her own unsupported weight for that long—she didn't seem to be suffering from shortness of breath.

He hated what she'd been through, what had almost happened, and it had damn well taken twenty years off his life seeing her swinging there unconscious. But tonight had also proven one thing beyond a shadow of a doubt.

Lillian was not the mole.

There was no way she could've faked what had happened tonight. No way she could've known that Jace would come through that door when he did. If he had been another minute later, just *one* minute, she would've been dead.

And if someone was leaving a suicide note

on her and trying to kill her, then Lillian Muir was not the mole.

The relief coursing through Jace now was almost as prominent as the relief of knowing she was alive after he'd seen her hanging there in the stairwell.

The proof of her innocence changed damn near everything for him. Every single reason he had for not giving in to the attraction that sparked between the two of them vanished as soon as he'd cut her down from the rope that had almost taken her life.

Jace couldn't stop himself from staring at her. She was alive and she was *innocent*.

"I'm not going to collapse, Eakin, so you can stop ogling me."

She had no idea why he couldn't drag his eyes away from her. She would soon.

If she would still have him.

They went straight to Derek's room. The sun was already coming up and he was awake. One look at Lillian's neck had his eyebrow raised, and he eased his door open farther for them to enter his room.

"You two get a little too excited with the sparring?" Derek asked.

Jace explained what happened, with Lillian filling in details, speaking as little as possible to protect her strained voice.

Jace sat down at the edge of the bed and pulled Lillian down beside him. She was starting to look a little paler. Was probably in a lot of pain.

"We told the building's security team about the break-in and unsecured window, but didn't give them much info about what happened to Lillian. I wasn't sure how you wanted to handle that. They brought in locals to process the scene and woke up every guard who's ever worked there to get them on-site."

Derek rubbed a hand across his face. "It's still not enough. I'll make a call. We're going to need further backup for the summit. We'll also need to move the summit to the secondary location. The bigwigs won't like it because it's not nearly as picturesque as city hall. Plus, we'll need to lock down an entirely new building." He turned to Lillian. "You need a hospital? You've been Tasered and strangled. Maybe you need to sit this event out."

Lillian stood. "I'm going to pretend I didn't even hear that. Bastard got a lucky shot, but it won't happen again. And I'm damn well not going to miss the LESS Summit. We're short-handed enough as it is."

The tough-person speech would've been much more convincing if her voice hadn't broken three times during it.

Jace couldn't help himself—his hand moved to her back to rub gentle circles. The fact that she didn't pull away both thrilled and worried him. "She's agreed to let the medic examine her. Then she'll be in my room."

He ignored Lillian's raised eyebrow.

Derek nodded. "I don't want to see either of you before thirteen hundred hours at the secondary location. We'll start the security lockdown and then prep for a run-through of the summit."

Jace and Lillian both stood and headed toward the door. Lillian turned back to Derek.

"You know what the mask means, right?" she croaked.

Derek rubbed the back of his neck. "It means Omega definitely has a mole, and that you would've known his face. We'll be sure to keep an eye on any reactions today when you show up. Because as far as that person knows, you died in that stairwell."

Jace's fists clenched. They'd come so damn close to that being the truth.

"Freihof is making his move, Derek. The summit is too good a target for him to pass up," Lillian whispered, her voice almost gone.

"And we'll be ready for him," Derek responded. "This is going to end. But first, go to the ER or at least go see the medic, get checked out. Then try to get some rest. Because you're right, we do need you. I have a feeling we're going to need all the help we can get."

Chapter Ten

Everybody needed to stop telling her to go to the ER. Jace. Derek. The medic. She was fine.

Lillian was angry as hell, but physically she would be fine. So the medic informing Jace—as if Jace was the boss of her—that she needed to be under constant supervision for the next twenty-four hours didn't do much for Lillian's temper.

"I'm fine," she muttered as they left the medic. "I don't need to stay in your room."

Jace looked at her calmly as he used the card key to open his hotel door. "Less than two hours ago you were unconscious from lack of oxygen. Your body is depleted. Exhausted. I understand you not wanting to go to the hospital, but please humor me on this. Stay with me."

His voice rolled over her like gentle waves, soothing her. Calming her.

But she also knew even soothing, calming water could drown her if she wasn't careful.

Lillian wanted to stay. And wanted to run. Maybe she was more injured than she thought, because she truly couldn't decide.

But finally she admitted to herself that the reason she wanted to run didn't have anything to do with proving her health and everything to do with how sexy Jace looked standing there against the wall in his jeans and shirt, holding the door open for her.

Holding the door open to the room that had one king-size bed as the main piece of furniture.

Lillian wasn't a coward, so she walked through the doorway, feeling Jace's hand at the small of her back as she did. Just like she'd felt it as they'd walked down the hall.

She knew she shouldn't read into it. He'd already made it quite clear he wasn't interested in anything more than a professional relationship. Working together. That was it. Being a friendly colleague was enough for her with everyone else. It would be enough with Jace, too.

Plus, she owed him. If he hadn't gotten there when he had, she'd definitely be dead now.

"Thank you for saving my life." She stood staring at the big bed for a moment before a thought occurred to her and she turned to him. "What were you doing at city hall anyway?"

She expected an immediate quip about insomnia or the problem with having a job that wasn't nine-to-five—with SWAT, probably the same as his time in the army, daytime and nighttime hours could run together.

Instead, Jace stepped closer. Directly into her definitely-more-than-just-professional space. There weren't a whole lot of things that threw Lillian off balance. This was one of them.

"I was looking for you."

Lillian took a slight step back, Jace's proximity a little too much for her system. "Okay. I'm glad you found me or else I'd—" She stopped, realization dawning. "You were following me?"

He nodded, features unreadable.

She tried to process the possible reasons why Jace would be following *her*. "Why?"

Now he stepped out of her space slightly, eyes shuttered. He paused so long she thought maybe he wasn't going to answer.

"I'm not just here to fill in for the SWAT team. I was also sent in by Ren McClement to look for the mole working with Freihof."

The mole. Lillian stepped away from Jace and walked over to the window that didn't provide much of a view. She leaned her forehead against the cool glass, taking in all the ramifications of Jace's statement.

"They sent you in because they think I'm the mole," she finally muttered. Somehow she'd always known there was a deeper purpose for Jace's sudden infiltration into the team.

She could hear him move closer behind her, but she didn't turn around. "They sent me in because Ren trusts me, they needed someone with a particular skill set and because...yes, they know there's a mole."

"And your past with me had nothing to do with them sending you in?"

Jace sighed. "No. They knew we'd known each other before when they asked me to join the team. You were one of the suspects. Although if it helps, your boss, that Steve Drackett guy, was adamant you weren't guilty."

"And you?" She hated the weakness in her voice as she whispered the question. Hated that the answer mattered so much to her. "Did *you* think I was guilty?"

She knew it was unfair. After what had happened between them twelve years ago—or what Jace *thought* had happened—expecting him to trust her carte blanche just wasn't fair. But God, how she wanted to believe he would find it impossible to conceive she was a traitor of that magnitude.

"Never mind," she said before he could answer. Before he could say the words she knew would tear her apart even though they shouldn't. "We don't really know each other, and what you did know about me wasn't complimentary. Of course you thought I was guilty."

She tried to give a lighthearted laugh, but it came out a brittle croak even to her own ears as she continued to stare out the window with no view. When he didn't respond, she continued, moving into a deeper register of her voice so it wouldn't crack. "We should get some rest like Derek said. Obviously we've got a ton of fortification work to do in a few hours now that we're moving to the secondary location."

"Tiger Lily…"

Damn it, he could *not* call her that. Not right now. Not when every part of her felt vulnerable.

She turned from the window but didn't meet his crystal eyes. She couldn't. Not right now. "You know what? I really am fine. I'm just going to head on up to my own room. I promise if I feel even the slightest bit—"

"No," he interrupted before she got any further. "I never thought you were guilty of treason. I didn't think it when Ren recruited me a couple of weeks ago. Hell, Lily, I didn't even think that when I felt the worst about you."

God, she wanted to believe that more than anything. "But yet, you came here, because of me. Followed me because you thought I might be up to something."

He took a step closer and ran a hand through

his brown hair, causing short pieces to stick up at crazy angles. "I came here because of you, yes. Because, despite everything, I've never been able to stop thinking about you. Because I wanted to put you—put the *past*—behind me once and for all."

That hurt almost as much as him thinking she was the mole. "Yeah, I can't blame you for that, either. Although I guess I'm glad you don't think I'm trying to kill my friends and betray my country, even if you don't like me personally."

His fingers gripped her upper arms. Not hard enough to hurt, and they both knew she had moves that could get her away from him if she wanted, but a firm enough touch to let her know that he was serious.

"It took me about three and a half minutes after seeing you to figure out that this heat between us was very definitely not in the past."

She couldn't look away from those eyes. "But what about the other day at HQ? You turning down my offer to come over? I thought you weren't interested."

He stepped closer. All Lillian could feel, smell, breathe…was Jace.

His volume dropped to a husky whisper. "I didn't want to be with you that way under false pretenses. I didn't want to have sex with you and then you think I had used it to get close to you to see if you were the mole."

"You *did* want me?" It had to be the near strangulation that made her voice so weak. So thready.

His hands moved up from her arms to cup her face. Her eyes closed and she breathed him in. He smelled of heat and desire and a scent that was pure male. Not just any male. *Jace.*

It had always been Jace. *Only* been Jace.

"Oh, hell yeah." His deep whisper sent chills across her skin. "But not with lies between us. And so while I hate what happened to you tonight, I'm also thankful for it. Because now there's no doubt in my mind you aren't the mole."

He was so close Lillian couldn't think clearly—all she could do was feel. And it felt so different than most interactions Lillian had with men. By this point of closeness she was normally checking out mentally. Fading away to some place in her mind that no one could touch. Even though her encounters with men weren't violent, her brain just wasn't able to process the intimacy.

But not now. She wanted to be here. With Jace. In every way.

She almost felt giddy. The desire coursing

through her veins like a fire was heady. She felt almost tipsy on it.

"I'm a little nervous about that smile," he said, lips so close to hers she could feel the hot sweetness of his breath. "You look like the cat that ate the canary."

"I just want to be with you." She couldn't help it, her smile grew wider as she pulled him closer. She wanted to revel in this feeling. "And it sounds like you want the same."

"Oh, you better believe it."

She let out a soft gasp as her body was pushed up against the window while his mouth came crashing down on hers. This kiss wasn't gentle or searching. Wasn't the kiss of the two teenagers they'd been.

It was hot. Forceful. Encompassing.

Everything about Jace demanded that Lillian's mind and focus stay here with him in the room. On him. On *them*.

Not that she wanted to be anywhere else. And hell if it wasn't the most authentic emotion she'd had in years. In twelve years.

Desire.

He kissed her with utter absorption, as if he couldn't get enough of her. Her fingers threaded in his hair as his hands slid down her back to her hips and he jerked her against him.

Lillian couldn't hold back the moan that broke free.

"I want you, Lily," he said against her lips.

Good, because she wanted him, too. In ways she thought had died long ago. She kept herself plastered against him as he picked her up by bending his knees and wrapping his arms around her hips. Then he lifted her and carried her to the bed.

He laid her down gently, without breaking the kiss, bringing his weight down on top of her. Lillian tensed.

She knew a man's form resting on her was one of her triggers—she and Grace had talked about it in depth in therapy—and Lillian waited for numbness to inch through her mind as it always did so she could fight it off.

But it didn't come.

All she could do was feel as Jace's lips moved over her jaw, taking special time to gently kiss down her injured throat. Finally he reached that most sensitive point, where her shoulder and neck met. He bit down gently and a soft cry escaped her.

She was feeling a million things. Numbness definitely was not one of them.

Jace's weight wasn't frightening, wasn't overwhelming her senses in a way that caused her mind to switch off in order to survive. That frightening place she'd barely survived as an eighteen-year-old wasn't looming in the distance.

Instead his weight was comfortable, as if her mind knew him, her body remembered him. Knew she was safe. And she was. Lillian knew that on every level.

Jace equaled safety.

As his hand ran down her body from her shoulder to her waist, unbuttoning her shirt as he went, she gripped his hair so she could see him face-to-face.

"I want you," she said, staring into those blue eyes that had once meant everything to her.

He gave her a half grin that stopped her heart and seemed to have a direct link to the most feminine parts of her. "You seem a little surprised by that statement."

"I just want to be here with you, all the way with you. Here and now." She knew she was being cryptic, that he couldn't possibly understand what she meant. And she definitely wasn't about to explain, especially not now.

But Jace just nodded. "Then stay with me, Tiger Lily. Here and now, in this bed. Just you and me." He bent down and brought his lips to hers again tenderly.

And she did. For the first time in twelve years she stayed—mentally—in a bed with a man. Not just any man. *Jace.* Experienced every kiss, every touch. Every moan and lick and sigh. Things she'd thought she was long past able to feel.

And found there was nowhere else she would rather be.

Chapter Eleven

"What the hell were you thinking, Freihof? If I hadn't come in and saved your ass, you'd be arrested right now."

Damien stared at "Guy Fawkes," his eyes narrowed to slits. The hell of it was, the younger man wasn't wrong. Damien had made a mistake. Had miscalculated. It didn't happen very often, but it had this morning.

It was the anniversary of his beloved Natalie's death. The day Omega Sector had swept in six years ago and taken her from him. Killed her in their heavy-handedness.

Damien hadn't planned to do anything about it. Moving on a day connected to Natalie would be too obvious. But he hadn't been able to stop himself.

They needed to pay.

He'd been toying with them for months, chasing and killing their loved ones so they could know the pain that he'd known from losing his Natalie.

But it was no longer enough. It was time for them to stop feeling the heartache of death and start feeling death itself. One by one... Groups... Damien didn't care which.

He just wanted them all to die.

Setting a trap in city hall—a bomb that would take out the entire SWAT team—had seemed like the perfect plan. Yes, it would've messed up some of Fawkes's destroy-all-of-law-enforcement plan, but Damien didn't care. He was tired of the game. Tired of Fawkes and his grand scheming. Tired of Omega Sector cheating death every time.

Tired of the same old story, so Damien was planning to turn some pages.

For Natalie. He could still picture her in his mind. Her blond hair and blue eyes. The perfect all-American girl. And she'd been all his. His most prized possession. Until they'd taken her away forever.

"Freihof!" Fawkes slammed his fist down on the table in the small apartment Damien had rented. "Are you listening to anything I'm saying? I took a big risk helping you and then again getting here to talk to you in person. You've probably ruined what I've taken months to set up."

The temptation to end Fawkes's life right now was almost more than Damien could bear. But it would be a mistake and Damien had already made one of those several hours ago. Fawkes was still useful and Damien needed to get his emotions under control.

A time and a place for everything. That was what he'd always told his beloved Natalie, and it was still true now.

"It won't happen again," Damien muttered through tight lips.

"It doesn't matter if it happens again!" Fawkes began pacing back and forth. "Thanks to your stunt, they're moving the summit to the secondary location. This changes everything for my plans. Networks I've painstakingly linked together for months ruined because you had to sneak in through a damn window in the middle of the night."

Damien watched the younger man pull at his own hair. Damien wouldn't have to kill him. He was going to give himself a stroke. "Fawkes, I will fix this."

"How?" Fawkes glared at him. "How exactly will you do that?"

"You let me worry about it. You concentrate on keeping your team from figuring out your grand scheme. From figuring out who you are."

Fawkes pulled at his hair again. "We have a

limited window, Damien. If all my systems are not aligned when LESS goes live in thirty-six hours, my plan fails. And city hall is the center of everything. Ground zero."

Damien nodded. "Like I said, I will make sure the summit is returned to the original location."

It would take work, but Damien already had a plan in mind.

"And Lillian Muir? She didn't die despite me stringing her up. I'm lucky I borrowed your mask because she would definitely be able to identify me, since she didn't die. And now she's even more suspicious."

"Yes, she's suspicious, but she's not suspicious of *you*. That's all that matters right now. She doesn't know who she saw entering that window. She doesn't know who strung her up in that hallway and she doesn't know any of the plans. Besides, I have something very special in store for her. And her boyfriend."

"Damn Eakin. Everybody accepted him into the SWAT team like he was some sort of god. I even saw Lillian making out with him in the parking lot last week."

The words fairly dripped with jealously. In just over a week, Eakin had done what Fawkes had been trying to do for months: make the team, get the girl. And, more importantly, gain respect. But pointing that out to the young Mr. Fawkes wasn't going to do any good.

Damien could see he'd been wrong to get so impatient. To want to jump straight to killing the SWAT team rather than torture them. They would still die, but first they would suffer.

Lillian Muir would especially. He had something special planned for her.

"I was wrong." Damien's voice was full of sincerity that for once he wasn't faking. "I shouldn't have tried to circumvent the plan. I will make sure we get back on track."

Fawkes nodded, somewhat appeased. "Good. What I'm doing is important, Damien. It's going to reshape law enforcement all over the world. The badge will mean something again. The badge will rule as it was meant to do from the beginning."

Ah, quoting the infamous "Manifesto of Change" once more. Fawkes constantly hid behind it, allowing it to mask his jealousy, fear and ineptitude. After all, killing thousands of people because you just couldn't make the SWAT team didn't have the same ring to it. But this manifesto, which he planned to release publicly after his massacre at the LESS Summit, made Fawkes feel more legitimate.

But Damien wasn't about to try to convince Fawkes of his own folly. He just nodded. "Change is necessary. There's a time and a place for everything. Omega Sector's time and place has come and gone. Together, we'll destroy them."

"There are things you don't know, Freihof. Plans I've made beyond what I've told you that even the precious SWAT team won't figure out."

"Are you sure they're not on to you?"

Fawkes just shrugged. "They suspect damn near everyone. But they'll never have proof. And soon they'll all be dead."

"Maybe it's time you let me know all the details of your plan. I'm sure I can help."

Fawkes grinned, but anger laced the expression rather than joy. Anyone who couldn't see that had to be blind. Then Fawkes began to tell Damien his entire plan. Damien just listened.

He realized that *everyone* had underestimated this young man.

And they all would burn.

When Jace woke up after a couple hours of sleep, Lillian was gone. He wasn't surprised. The medic had told him to keep an eye on her to make sure she was okay.

Jace had kept a very close eye on her. On *all* of her. For hours.

It was like they were trying to cram twelve

years of not making love into a few short hours. *Intense* was an applicable term for the last few hours they'd spent in bed, but would be an understatement.

Mind-blowing, earth-shattering, game-changing—those would be closer to the truth.

Jace wasn't so naive as to think that everything was perfect between him and Lillian just because they'd had some awesome sex. There were still a lot of years and a huge betrayal between them. He'd told himself—and her—that he was going to let the situation with Daryl be left in the past, but he had to admit he wasn't one-hundred-percent sure he was there yet.

Lily had seemed as enraptured in their lovemaking as he had been. She'd actually seemed a little surprised at their connection. At the heat. Had mentioned more than once how she wanted him, as if the notion caught her a little off guard.

A heat that all-encompassing after twelve years *was* a little surprising. Of course they'd had heat at the beginning, too.

That hadn't stopped Jace from finding Lily in his brother's arms a few days later. So there was no reason to think something similar wouldn't happen again. He needed to remember that. Keep his head on straight when it came to her.

Mind-blowing sex? No problem. Jace would partake as often as possible during this mission.

Giving Lily a piece of his heart? Absolutely not. He couldn't allow this to become more than a burn-the-sheets-off-the-bed sexual encounter between two friendly colleagues who would go their separate ways.

He brutally squashed the niggling voice that tried to tell him that Lillian Muir had always held a piece of his heart.

Jace showered and grabbed a bite to eat before dressing in full SWAT gear. He knew Lillian would meet at the secondary location at 1300 hours, like Derek had requested. Knew she would act as if nothing had happened, in both her near-death experience and the passion between the two of them. Lillian was never going to be one to wear her heart—or her weaknesses—on her sleeve.

Jace would be professional, too. Because although he definitely planned to have Lillian back in his bed, they couldn't deny that there was a very real threat here at the LESS Summit. Freihof and his crony might not have succeeded in making it look like Lillian was the mole, and taken her out of the picture, but that didn't mean they would turn their backs on an opportunity to do damage.

By surviving, Lillian had just upped the ante for whatever they had planned.

Omega would need to be ready.

Chapter Twelve

Jace was making his way to the federal building serving as the secondary location when the call came through. The entire team was to stop what they were doing and head to the lobby of the adjoining building. Some sort of elevator emergency.

He met Lillian as she was running from the federal building. Roman Weber and Saul Poniard were just two steps behind.

"Why the hell are we being brought in for a stuck elevator? Why didn't they call the fire department?" Jace asked as they ran, having to dodge picketers holding signs and chanting. The summit didn't start until tomorrow, but the public and news crews were already out in full force.

"Maybe the fire department has more on their plate than they can handle. But you can believe that Derek wouldn't call the entire team from our current assignment if we weren't needed."

Jace already knew that they were needed. It was confirmed a few minutes later as they all met up in the lobby. People were rushing by them, not screaming in panic, but not calm, either.

The presence of a SWAT team wasn't helping. People could tell something was wrong.

Derek spoke fast. "As we knew, the summit is bringing out the crazies. We've got four different bomb threats across the city, all tied to elevators. People are stranded in them all, and the guy is threatening to detonate all the bombs in thirty minutes if he doesn't get his demands met."

Saul cursed next to Jace. The ugly word very neatly summarized how he was feeling also.

"A police negotiator is talking with the bomber, criminal psychiatrist assisting, but they both have already signaled that they think the bomber has every intention of killing people today. Wants the attention, not the three million dollars he's demanding. Local police is spread thin, so we're working this building."

Now muttered curses could be heard all the way around.

"What's the plan, Derek? If he's going to blow it, let's get the people out before he can,"

Lillian said, her small body already strumming with energy.

"Elevator is caught between the sixteenth and seventeen floors. Eight people inside. We're going to have to jimmy the door open and pull the people out. But our clock is limited, especially if this guy is wanting to kill people solely for the attention. We have twenty-two minutes exactly."

The entire team set their watches. Anybody who was crazy enough to plant a bomb that would kill innocent people wasn't someone who could be trusted to keep his word, but until they had other intel they would move as if they had twenty-two minutes.

"Roman, Ashton, you need to help clear the stairwells and keep people moving without panic. Especially if this thing blows." Both men nodded and moved toward the main stairwell.

"Jace, Lillian, Saul," Derek continued, "you're with me."

The entire team sprinted to the stairwell and up the sixteen flights, the benefits of their daily physical training kicking in. Jace worried for a moment that Lillian might not be able to keep up because of her injuries, but she never faltered.

Less than three minutes later they were in the hall of the sixteenth floor. Derek used the elevator-emergency drop key to release the outer doors and pried them open.

Immediately they found the elevator car was over three quarters of the way up from the building doorway. There was no way anyone would be able to fit through the small space. They would have to go to the next floor.

Jace let out a curse, doing the rough math in his head based on the height of the stairwell.

"What?" Lillian asked.

"That car is too high on this floor to get them out here, but based on the height of the ceilings and stairwell, it's going to be damn tight trying to get them out on the next floor as well."

"We've got to try," Derek said. "We're down to seventeen minutes."

Immediately everyone sprinted to the next floor. The emergency drop key was reapplied on both the outer and inner doors and Jace's theory was unfortunately proven true. There was less than fifteen inches of space for the trapped passengers to fit through.

The passengers inside were talking, but weren't hysterical. They probably thought it was just a malfunction rather than a deliberate act of terror.

"This is the SWAT team," Derek called out. "We're going to pry open the door. Please stand back."

A small cheer went up from inside the car as force was applied to the inner door…until the door was pried open and the passengers could see the small space they'd have to get through.

"Can't you get the elevator up or down farther to give us more room? Some of us aren't going to fit."

Fourteen minutes.

The team looked to Derek. Nobody wanted to cause a panic, but they were going to have to work pretty damn fast to get all eight people out of there in time. And the guy who spoke up was right, it was going to be tough for some of them to fit. Jace himself would have a hard time.

But not everybody. Before they knew it, a petite woman was being hefted by someone in the elevator and was easily sliding through the fifteen-inch opening. One down, seven to go.

"Good!" Derek called out. "Send up as many people as you can."

Two more women and a skinny teenager were sent through next. Jace helped the team pull them out. Lillian, knowing her lack of upper body strength was a hindrance rather than a help, particularly after what she'd been through less than twelve hours ago, scooted out of the way. She eased her head inside the elevator car to get a good look at the remaining four passengers.

When she pulled back out, she was shaking her head, lips pursed. Her eyes met Jace's, but she spoke to Derek. "That last guy isn't going to fit," she said softly so only the team could hear.

"He's going to have to," Derek muttered, pulling passenger number six through.

"He's three hundred pounds, Derek," Lillian replied. "There's no way he's going to make it through that opening, even if we could pull him up."

Before Jace knew what was happening, Lillian gracefully poured herself through the opening and into the elevator car.

"Muir, what are you doing?" Saul yelled.

Jace met Derek's eyes as they hoisted the seventh passenger—a large man who barely fit through the opening—out of the elevator. Jace already knew what Lillian was doing. She knew they weren't going to be able to get the last guy out, so she was looking for other solutions to the problem.

"She's searching for the device," he muttered to Derek.

"What device?" the man they'd just pulled through asked. "A *device*? Like a bomb?"

The other people gasped and the elderly lady grasped her chest. "There's a bomb?"

Derek and Jace ignored them. "Disarming is

the only option if we can't get everyone out," Jace said. "I'm going in with her."

Jace glanced at his watch. Eight minutes.

The civilians were now crying. Derek turned to Saul. "Lead them down the stairs."

The older woman gripped her chest again, her breathing ragged. Jace studied her briefly before turning back to Derek. "Saul isn't going to be able to get them all down."

Derek nodded. "I'll help him. You're the explosives expert. I sure as hell hope you can work a miracle."

Jace did, too.

Derek stepped closer. "But if you can't, then you make sure the body count is as low as possible, you understand? One is bad enough. We don't need to make it three."

"Agreed."

"Lillian won't see it that way."

"Lillian already almost died once in the past twelve hours. I'm not going to let it happen again now."

Derek nodded curtly and moved to help the other civilians. Jace lowered himself into the elevator.

"What the hell is going on here?" the man too big to fit through the opening said loudly, sweat pouring down his face. "Why is SWAT here rather than the fire department?"

Lillian was ignoring him. She was using an electric screwdriver to open panels on the elevator, searching for the bomb.

"Fire department is busy in other parts of the city, sir," Jace responded to the man.

"Well, then get a damn elevator repairman out here. Whatever this girlie is doing can't be helping. A woman with power tools always makes me nervous. One in a broken elevator is downright terrifying."

Now Jace understood why Lily was ignoring the sexist jackass.

She turned to him. "These panels are all clear. Nothing. I didn't think it would be here, but it was worth a shot, since that would've been the easiest access." She pointed to the roof panels. "Hoist me up."

They both ignored the man, who was still spouting off from the corner. Jace linked his fingers by his knees and Lillian immediately stepped into his hands. He lifted her until she could reach the ceiling panels and unscrew them. A few moments later she grasped the sides of the opening and lifted herself through.

Her muttered curse told him the news was not good.

"Tell Derek to let the other locations know there's a primary device on the main cable and a second one on the emergency break," she said down to him.

"Device?" the guy yelled. "What kind of device?"

They ignored him again.

Jace relayed the message to the team leader, then continued, "This is beyond my pay grade, Derek. No way I'm going to be able to defuse this in time."

The big guy went crazy, became livid. "There's a bomb up there? Don't you think you should've told me about that, you bitch?"

What was it with this sexist freak? Jace pointed a finger right in the middle of his chest. "You know what? There's only one person stuck in this elevator without a way out. It's not me and it's definitely not her." He pointed up to where Lillian was on the roof. "So shut the hell up and help us save your life."

The man shut up and nodded, thankfully.

"Lillian, I'm coming up." Jace crouched and jumped, catching the opening in the ceiling and pulling himself the rest of the way through. Lily was shining her flashlight on the small explosive device.

"Four minutes." He shone his own light at the secondary device on the emergency brake.

"Hell, I don't even know what I'm looking at, Jace. The entire team knows that explosives aren't my specialty. I don't have the patience for it. Tell me what I need to do."

Jace studied the bomb in front of him. There wasn't time to inspect both separately. He would have to work on his and walk Lillian through hers at the same time. "Tell me what you see."

What was in front of him was a hot mess. Definitely not something crafted with care. It almost seemed to have been thrown together.

Derek's voice came in through his earpiece. "Report, Jace. You're running out of time."

"This device isn't what I was expecting, especially for someone we would've thought had been planning this since the summit was announced. This device is almost haphazard."

"The other three buildings couldn't find any explosive devices in the elevators. Looks like the bomber was just using those as decoys to spread rescue personnel more thinly."

"It worked," Jace muttered, still studying the messy IED in front of him. "Something about this whole thing is off, Derek."

"That's not going to stop us from being less dead in three minutes if we don't get this figured out," Lillian quipped.

"You focus on the task at hand," Derek's voice said in his ear. "We'll figure out what doesn't fit later."

"Roger that," Jace muttered, clicking off his transmission. "Lil, I need you to figure out the four main parts of your bomb. Main charge, a trigger switch, the ignitor and the power source for the switch."

"Okay."

"We've got to separate the trigger switch from its power source."

Lillian blew out a frustrated breath. "So this is going to be more than just cut the red wire or the blue wire?"

"Actually, believe it or not, it is a case of just cutting a wire. But if your IED is anything like mine, it's a mess. Bomber didn't take much care with this explosive. But like you said, it will still get us just as dead."

"We're under two minutes, Jace. Which wire am I supposed to cut?"

They both heard the guy in the elevator start crying, promising God he would go to church every day for the rest of his life if he survived this.

"Tell Him you'll stop making sexist remarks, too. Maybe that will help," Lillian called down to him.

Jace grinned. This woman.

He couldn't wait to get her back in his bed. All the thoughts about keeping his distance from her seemed ridiculous now.

The bomb was messy, but still cleverly put together. Not easily disarmed. Jace gently pried the battery—the trigger switch's power source—away from the main charge. He barely saw the tiny aluminum wire attached to the bottom of the red wire—the one that would need to be cut to separate the trigger from its power source.

A fail-safe. If that tiny wire got cut by accident—by someone who didn't see it—the explosive would detonate. The person who built this might have been in a hurry, but he was very smart.

They were in serious trouble.

"Lil, you need to go."

She didn't even look up. "Like hell I will. Especially not without you."

"Negotiator was right. Whoever rigged this didn't plan on anyone surviving here today, no matter what demands he gave."

Guy below them began crying louder.

"Is it possible to defuse it?" she asked. Their eyes met across the roof of the elevator. Hers were calm, like his. Lillian could handle it.

"Yes, but it's tricky."

She grinned. "Tricky is my middle name, Eakin. What do I do?"

He quickly explained about the aluminum wire, the need to separate it gently from the other wire that had to be cut. It was glued and nearly impossible to do. Just getting the device in front of him defused would take all his time. There was no way he'd be able to help Lillian with hers.

"Okay, I see it." She muttered a curse. "I really don't like whoever put this damn thing together."

"You found the adhesive, I see. Forty-five seconds."

"Yep, damn it. Wanna race?"

Jace couldn't keep from chuckling. Lily. God, if he had to go out, there was no one else he'd rather go with.

Guy inside was wailing now.

Jace carefully eased his blade through the tiny wire, using the utmost caution not to cut the aluminum wire around it. He took in a breath to focus and then made the final cut.

"Clear," he breathed.

He looked over at Lillian. They had less than fifteen seconds. Jace stayed where he was. The best thing he could do now was let her do her job. Trust her to do it. And he did, he realized. She was crouched there, small flashlight now in her mouth pointing down at the device, completely focused on the task at hand.

That was the Lillian he'd always known. Able to handle anything.

C'mon, Tiger Lily. Save our lives.

He'd no more than finished the thought when she looked up, grabbed the flashlight out of her mouth and grinned.

"Clear."

Chapter Thirteen

"Canceling the LESS Summit is not an option," Congresswoman Christina Glasneck said an hour later, since she had decided to attend the SWAT debriefing to provide her own input. Colorado was her state and LESS was her baby.

And she wasn't happy.

"Omega Sector is supposed to be made up of the best agents the country has available for service. So, can you handle this or not?"

Lillian would've told the woman off, but Derek remained unflappable. "Yes, ma'am. We can handle it."

Congresswoman Glasneck tapped a heeled foot as she leaned back against the conference-room chair. "So we had a break-in at city hall last night and a bombing scare today. Are the two incidents related?"

Lillian was glad she'd worn a high-necked dry-fit shirt under her gear. The bruising around her neck was extensive. And although

Derek had let the team know she had thwarted some sort of break-in at the City and County Building, he hadn't provided many details.

Although someone—probably someone sitting inside this very room—knew many more details about last night than they were letting on.

"It's too early to ascertain with any certainty," Derek responded to Glasneck. "But as of right now, we have nothing to suggest the two events are related."

Lillian glanced over at Jace. His face was stoic, as were the faces of the entire team. The congresswoman had requested everyone be here for this meeting, which wasn't normal protocol and was a waste of time. There was a crap ton of more useful things the team could be doing than sitting here listening to a lecture from someone who wanted to feel like she had a finger on the pulse of law enforcement.

It gave Lillian a new respect for Derek, who had to sit through these types of meetings all the time.

"As you know," Congresswoman Glasneck continued, "LESS has been my project from the beginning. I pushed it through Congress to get the necessary funding." She looked over at Philip Carnell. "Mr. Carnell, you've been instrumental in the setup of the system, and I know a number of other members of Omega Sector have worked tirelessly across the country to make sure this system happens. I think you helped, too, didn't you, Mr. Poniard?"

Saul nodded. But Carnell, true to form, barely even acknowledged the congresswoman's words. He sat with his arms crossed over his chest.

Derek nodded. "We all understand the importance of LESS, Congresswoman. And of protecting the summit. None of us want it to be canceled, but we do need to decide on a final location. Right now it seems the primary and secondary locations have been compromised."

The congresswoman's lips thinned. "I agree that this federal building is out. After the elevator incident today, I'm sure no one wants to place a large group of VIPs here. But I disagree about city hall. That's one of the oldest buildings in Denver. Iconic."

Again, Lillian wanted to jump in and argue why the outer appearance of a building should be the last thing they were concerned about. This was why Derek had told the entire team to just keep quiet unless they were asked a direct question.

"It is a beautiful building," Derek conceded. "But the fact is, it was compromised. We had eyes on someone infiltrating the building, but that person got away."

"I'm not trying to tell you how to do your job, Agent Waterman, but isn't it true that we have no credible intel on what the person who slipped into that window was doing? We don't know if the perpetrator had anything to do with today's bomb scare, nor do we have intel suggesting it was someone with nefarious purposes aimed at the LESS Summit. As a matter of fact, a broken cash box in the café on the first floor suggests it might have been a burglary. Perhaps even a juvenile."

Lillian had had enough. "Like hell. That was no kid I fought last night—"

Derek held out a hand and Lillian quieted.

"Agent Muir is one of our top team members, Congresswoman Glasneck. I trust her implicitly. If she says it was an adult she fought, even though the perpetrator was wearing a mask, I believe her."

Glasneck glanced over at Lillian and gave her a slight nod. "I appreciate any woman who works and fights in the midst of what is primarily a man's world. I know a little about that. So I'm honestly not trying to be disrespectful when I say that I'm sorry the perpetrator was able to get the best of you in a fight."

"Guy had the help of a Taser," Jace said.

"That's just about the only way someone would get a jump on Lillian otherwise," Saul insisted. Everyone else nodded.

At least Lillian knew her team felt she was fully capable of taking care of herself in a situation. Derek hadn't provided any details about what had happened after the guy had Tasered her. Lillian didn't know if Congresswoman Glasneck knew, either.

Not that it mattered. The long and short of it was, Lillian had gotten her ass handed to her. And almost died because of it.

"I'm sure that's true," Glasneck said. "But the point is, Agent Muir wasn't in any shape to ascertain the perpetrator's true intent. It quite possibly could've been a burglar she stumbled in on."

"The facts of the situation let us know that it was definitely not a simple break-in," Derek said.

Lillian knew he was trying to keep the details about the "suicide" note confidential.

"Suffice it to say we have definite cause to believe the person who broke in was someone who knew Lillian. Was probably a terrorist named Damien Freihof that has been plaguing Omega Sector for months."

The older woman huffed out a breath. "But you have no proof of that."

Derek remained steady. "No, no proof. But we also know, based on evidence left at the scene, it was someone acquainted with Agent Muir. So although it may not have been Damien Freihof, it also means it wasn't a simple break-in."

Derek definitely wasn't mentioning the mole was probably sitting somewhere inside this room. That would not instill confidence.

"Okay, it wasn't a burglar." The congress-woman held out her hands in front of her. "But you can agree that maybe it was someone with a vendetta against Agent Muir. And that it had nothing to do with the summit itself."

Derek nodded shortly. "Yes. That is possible. But I can tell you that hosting the summit at the Denver City and County Building, no matter how picturesque, is a mistake. Someone wanting to attack the summit has had too much time to prepare. Moving to an unknown secondary location will put any potential attacker back at square one."

"Also puts us back at square one," Carnell muttered. "Finding a suitable replacement, getting all the plans, figuring out the details… that's going to take time we don't have, considering the summit is tomorrow."

A lot of that work would fall on Carnell because of his computer skills, so Lillian couldn't blame him for his frustration. Neither option—sticking with the building they were familiar with, but so was their enemy, or moving to an entirely unknown place—was very good.

"Agent Waterman, we have dozens of important people from all over the country coming to witness the initialization of the LESS system. And that doesn't include the thousands of other government officials and law-enforcement officers who will be watching from their stations as LESS goes live."

"We're all aware of the VIPs, Congresswoman. You're one of them."

"I'm least of them," the woman said, and laughed. "But thank you. I don't want this summit to take place in some back room across town just because of what might be a potential threat, but might not be. The very purpose of LESS is to show terrorists and criminals that law enforcement will not cower. We will face terror and crime head-on, standing together."

It was a rousing speech, one the woman obviously already had planned before this debrief had started. But Lillian could see her point. Looking around, she saw it was obvious the rest of the team could, too.

"Yeah, boss," Saul said. "Let's prove what we can do. What law enforcement can do. We don't cower."

Lillian almost had to roll her eyes again, but she couldn't fault the newbie's enthusiasm. Evidently, neither could Derek.

"All right, Congresswoman, since we don't have conclusive evidence of any upcoming attack, we'll keep the summit at city hall. But you have to understand that if intel changes, so will security plans. I won't put people at undue risk just for some photo ops."

Glasneck nodded. "Agreed. And I wouldn't expect you to. Now, I'm sure your team has better things to do than sit around and talk to me. I'll let you get to your business and I'll handle mine." The woman nodded, then left, her aides and Secret Service agent, on special loan for the summit, following behind.

Derek turned to the team, who was mostly lined up across the wall. "Okay, people, you heard the lady, we're back at the City and County Building. We will be resweeping it from top to bottom. I know it's nobody's favorite job, but we'll be doing it anyway. We'll be checking every damn nook and cranny until we know it's secure."

Saul was already nodding enthusiastically, like he couldn't wait to get to it. That would pass. It was something Saul didn't understand and it might be part of the reason why he'd never been chosen for a permanent part of the team. He wanted action all the time. But a lot of SWAT work was boring. Routine. Knowing how to handle the boredom was just as important as knowing how to handle the action. Maybe even more so because there wasn't any outlet for the boredom.

You either figured out how to handle it or got another job.

And now they had a lot of hours of tedious work in front of them. Made even more difficult since they didn't know if the mole was someone on the team. It was the other reason why Derek hadn't pushed harder against Congresswoman Glasneck for a new location for the summit. Because if one of their inner team members was the mole, changing locations wasn't going to protect them against an attack.

Nothing would.

LILLIAN STOOD TO join the rest of the team as they began to exit the conference room. Dizziness assailed her and she grabbed the back of a nearby chair to steady herself.

Jace was immediately next to her. "You okay?" He said it softly enough that no one else could hear and blocked the rest of the room from being able to see her. He was protecting her in the way he knew would mean the most to her.

Just like he'd trusted her to get the bomb defused earlier. If he hadn't, if he'd tried to rush in and take over for her, they'd both be dead. Them and that poor sexist bastard who'd been hyperventilating in the elevator.

Jace was strong enough not to feel threatened by her strength. He also knew her well enough to know she wouldn't want him fawning over her in this moment. That the best way he could help was by being a human shield to keep others from seeing her in a moment of weakness.

How could this man still be so perfect for her after so many years?

Lillian couldn't help it, she breathed in his scent as he stood so close to her. Sweat. Male.

Jace.

They were both still in full tactical gear from the elevator incident, so being too close wasn't even possible. But he was still the sexiest thing she'd ever seen.

"Lil?" he asked again when she didn't answer. "You okay?"

"Yeah." She nodded, clearing her voice when the word came out hoarse from the earlier trauma. "Just stood up too fast. Plus, it's already been a long day and it's about to get longer."

"You need a break?"

She felt his hand on her elbow.

"Maybe we shouldn't have used all your downtime for…other activities this morning."

Lillian smiled. She couldn't help it. She couldn't even pretend that what had happened in the hotel room between them was anything short of spectacular. "I liked the *other activities.*"

Jace winked at her and she felt heat zip through her. "Good. Because I'm hoping to show you some variations on those *other activities* later."

More steady now, she turned with Jace and followed the others out of the room. Derek joined them, shooting off assignments as he went. Denver PD would be sending backup to help with the initial securing of the building, but someone from Omega Sector would be double-checking every floor. And then a different person from the Omega team would check it again.

To an outsider it would look like diligence, having two separate team members looking for security leaks. And maybe it was diligence. But it was also to try to protect themselves from the mole.

As they walked back over to the City and County Building from the federal building, the crowds of people were steadily getting bigger. Lillian noticed Philip Carnell was walking alone. Not unusual—most people didn't want to converse with Carnell unless they had to.

But Lillian noticed he was walking stiffly, as if he was in pain. A few moments later he moved the material of his long-sleeve shirt— and she saw a bruise on his forearm.

Right where bruises would've been if he'd blocked some kicks and punches in a fight.

Lillian tried to focus on the details of her fight with the masked man. Could it have been Carnell? She didn't think Carnell was physically capable of the fighting skill level of the man she'd gone up against.

But heaven knew Carnell was brilliant enough to have been faking his weaknesses. The guy had a mind like a computer—he could've figured out long ago that he needed to appear weak physically to the team to throw suspicion off himself.

The masked man she'd fought had been roughly the same height. She'd thought he was more muscular than Carnell, but he tended to wear such loose clothing at Omega Sector that Lillian couldn't say for certain what his actual physique was.

Was this the bastard who had attacked her, Tasered her, then strung her up in the hallway, leaving her to die?

"Carnell, wait up." She marched over to him

as they reached the steps to city hall. He slowed slightly, looking at her with irritation.

"What do you want?"

The guy really was a jerk.

"Where'd you get that bruise on your arm?"

Carnell's eyes narrowed. "None of your damn business."

She grabbed his wrist. "Is it new? It's pretty purple. Hasn't turned green, so it must have happened in the last twenty-four hours."

Carnell snatched his arm back and pushed down his sleeve. "What do you want, Muir? I'm trying to work out the best way to split up the team to be most effective in securing the building. I don't have time for your little power play."

Before he could move farther away, Lillian had his left wrist in her hand. She twisted it, to bring his arm around his back, and pushed him against the metal banister of the stairway, her other hand reaching up and applying pressure at his throat. "Do I look like I'm playing anything, Carnell? Where the hell did you get the bruise on your forearm and why are you walking so stiffly? Do you have other bruises? Maybe take a kick to the ribs? A punch to the sternum?" All had been blows she'd delivered during her fight.

"Are you crazy?" Carnell yelled, eyes wide. "Let go of me!"

"Mind if I get in on the fun?"

Lillian heard Jace's voice just over her shoulder.

"He's got bruises on his forearm, Jace. Looks a lot like defensive wounds. And he's walking funny, like he got in a fight recently. Pretty suspicious, don't you think?"

"What the hell are you talking about?" Carnell spat out.

"Let him go, Lillian." This time it was Derek over her other shoulder.

"Derek—"

"I understand your concerns," Derek continued. "But let him go so he can talk."

Reluctantly Lillian took her hand from Carnell's throat and released his wrist. She didn't lower her guard, ready to move quickly if he went to draw a weapon or run.

Carnell looked over at Derek. "Did you see that? She attacked me for no reason. She's emotionally unstable."

Derek turned to the rest of the team. "Everyone else inside. You know your initial assignments, so get to them."

The rest of the team dispersed, although they looked like they wanted to stay.

"Where are the bruises from, Philip?" Derek asked once everyone was gone.

"I don't have to tell you," Carnell sputtered. "It's none of your damn business."

Lillian felt the heat of Jace's body directly behind her shoulder. "It is when it seems like some of your bruises match some of the hits taken by the guy who attacked Lillian late last night."

"Know anything about that, Carnell?" Lillian asked.

"What? No. I wouldn't attack you, Muir. Why the hell would I want to fight you? Everybody knows you could kick my ass. Everybody on the team could kick my ass, that's why I'm not an official SWAT member, remember?"

She narrowed her eyes at him. "Maybe you've just been acting like you couldn't fight. Throw suspicion off yourself."

"Suspicion of what? Me being the mole?"

"You know anything about that?" Derek asked.

He rolled his eyes. "You said there was no proof, but we all know there's a mole somewhere inside Omega. Somebody's helping Damien Freihof. But it's not me."

"Where'd you get the bruises, Carnell?" Lillian asked again. He certainly had the know-how and the smarts to be the mole. She didn't like to think that he'd beaten her in a fight, but it was possible.

"It's none of your damn business, but if you must know, I got a little roughed up by a couple of guys outside a bar last night."

Derek's eyebrows shot up. "What the hell were you doing at a bar when we're all on duty?"

Carnell snorted loudly. "I wasn't actually at the bar. I don't need a lot of sleep, so I was walking around town. I passed a bar as a couple of guys were coming out and I may have made a disparaging remark about the team on their sports jerseys. They didn't like it and I took a few punches."

Lillian looked over at Jace and then at Derek—they both wore matching bemused looks. None of them had a problem imagining Carnell getting beat on because he ran his mouth to the wrong people.

"I blocked one punch," he continued, "but still took a couple to the midsection. Luckily some other people came out of the bar, and I left while they were distracted."

Was he telling the truth? It seemed like it, but Lillian didn't know the younger man well enough to know. And she had to admit after everything that had happened in the last twelve hours—attacked, almost killed, earth-shattering lovemaking, almost killed again by a bomb this time—she was not at her sharpest.

"Can anybody vouch for you?" Derek asked. "Your whereabouts?"

"I'm sure if I could track down the jerks who jumped me they'd be glad to try to finish the job. But no, other than them I wasn't really socializing. Why the hell do you guys care anyway? I'm sick of being everyone's punching bag. First strangers and now my so-called teammates. Don't we have enough bad guys to concentrate on?"

"Go on in the building and get set up, Philip," Derek said. "We'll be inside in just a minute."

Carnell was still muttering to himself as he left and walked into the building. Lillian wiped a hand across her face as she turned to look at Jace and Derek.

"That very well could be our mole," Jace said, taking a step closer to her. "God knows he's smart enough to be."

"The guy you fought knew what he was doing, right, Lillian?" Derek asked.

"Yes. If it wasn't for Carnell's bruises, I would never have suspected he could've been the guy that got the jump on me."

Jace shook his head. "It could've been a second person. You don't know."

"Following Carnell stealthily, trying to see what he was up to without his knowledge, probably would've been the better plan than a hostile confrontation."

Derek's tone was completely neutral, but Lillian knew she'd made a huge tactical error in what she'd just done. "I'm sorry, Derek. I screwed up."

"You're tired, in pain and your judgment is being affected."

Again neutral. But Lillian still felt like she might vomit. "I—"

Derek held out a hand to stop her. "You'll go back to the hotel and rest for twelve hours before coming back on duty."

What? "You need me here. You need every man you can get."

"I'll need you more over the next two days as the summit swings into full gear. So get the downtime you need so you can come back in top shape." Derek put his hand on her shoulder. "Lillian, if anyone else had been through what you had yesterday and today, you would encourage me to give them the time they needed to regroup. This is not a reflection on your ability. This is about keeping the team running as efficiently as possible."

She knew Derek was right, but it still sucked. She felt like she'd let him down. Let the team down.

"We're going to be on rotating shifts from

now until the summit is completed," Derek continued. "You're just taking the first down shift."

"Okay." Damn it.

Derek looked over at Jace. "You two are on my very short list of people I know I can trust. I'm going to need you firing on all cylinders." Derek squeezed her shoulder, then turned and walked into city hall.

She looked at Jace. "I guess I'm grounded and am going to take a nap."

He smiled. "I guess I shouldn't have kept you up this morning."

She rubbed her eyes. "Then we can agree that me acting like a complete moron and losing us the upper hand with the potential mole is all your fault."

"You reacted. It happens."

Lillian rubbed her eyes again. "Derek's right. I'm tired. My judgment is impaired."

He pulled her closer by her tactical vest. "Then do what the man says and get some rest."

She grabbed her extra hotel card key out of a Velcro pocket, held it up to Jace and told him her room number. "Join me later if your downtime happens to coincide with mine?"

She didn't want to think too hard about the butterflies she got inside her chest when he nodded and smiled. He kissed her on the tip of

her nose, turned and jogged into the building.
She couldn't tear her eyes off him.

She was in so much trouble.

Chapter Fourteen

It had been a long-ass day. Jace had worked with the others, helping to confirm the security of the Denver City and County Building. Derek had used Jace mostly to double-check particularly vulnerable places, since he knew Jace couldn't be the mole. There were definitely no unsecured windows or doors in this building now.

For the moment. Jace and Derek both knew the mole could come back and change that situation.

Jace had left a few markers—invisible to anyone but him—in areas he thought would be potential targets for Freihof or the mole. These markers, generally made of pretty innocuous items like tape and string, would let him know if windows or doors had been opened or tampered with when he went back and checked them. Derek was doing the same, trying to keep the LESS Summit secure and catch the mole at the same time.

They both knew fighting a war on two fronts was the surest way to lose. But right now it was their only option, especially with someone potentially working against them.

Was it Carnell? The bruises were suspicious. Even in the short time Jace had been around he'd noticed the man was always angry. Always talking about elitist problems in Omega Sector and the lack of pedigree in law enforcement in general. Definitely corresponded with some of the "Manifesto of Change" document Ren McClement had shown Jace back in his office in DC.

But Lillian had said the man she'd followed in the window had put up a pretty good fight before she'd been Tasered. Jace had difficulty believing she couldn't drop Carnell in under five seconds flat.

Hell, she could drop Jace in under ten if he didn't use every skill he had.

So neither he nor Derek thought Carnell was the man who'd fought and strung up Lillian last night.

Speaking of, that damn key card had been burning a hole in his pocket for the past seven hours. Jace had purposely forced himself not to think about Lillian, to focus on the task at hand as he worked. The job required his focus, and Lillian needed time to rest.

Seeing how upset she'd been with herself over how she'd handled Carnell had been painful. Derek had been right to give her the first down shift. Everybody had their limits. Lillian's body and mind had evidently reached hers.

Jace damn well hoped she'd spent the last few hours sleeping. Now that Derek had told him to break, Jace planned to wake her up in the most pleasurable way possible, then hopefully talk her back into another nap afterward. In his arms. Both of them naked.

Full-on grin covering his face, Jace found himself all but jogging back to the hotel. It was already dark again. He should be exhausted, but as he peeled away his tactical gear and showered, all he could think about was getting to Lillian.

She'd given him her room key. And while that wasn't exactly an engagement ring, Jace recognized it for what it was: a statement of trust.

Nothing about Lillian then or now suggested she gave her trust easily.

He used the key to enter her room. It was dark inside except for the light on in the bathroom with the door cracked. Evidently Lillian didn't like the dark.

"Lil, you awake?" he said softly, looking at her small form huddled in the bed. She'd kicked part of the blankets off, showing off one leg. She was dressed in just an oversize T-shirt and her underwear.

It was possibly the sexiest thing Jace had seen in his whole life.

"Lil?" he said again, moving closer.

"Hey," she said sleepily, turning toward him. "What took you so long?"

It was all the invitation Jace needed. He stripped his shirt over his head, pulled off his sweats and climbed into the bed with her. God, he had been purposely *not* thinking about this all day, knowing he'd never be able to focus on the task at hand if he did.

Bracing his elbows on either side of her head, he lowered his weight on her. "Hey, sexy."

He brought his lips to hers, easing them open. She shifted beneath him, a soft sigh escaping her. He grabbed her under one of her knees and hooked her leg up over his hips, bringing their bodies closer together. He couldn't stop the moan that escaped him. Didn't even try.

He ran one hand up and down the outer part of her thigh on the leg wrapped around his hip. His other gripped her hair, tilting her head back so he could kiss her more fully. He felt her fingernails grip into his shoulders and groaned again.

His lips moved down her jaw to her throat, to that place right under her ear that he knew was so sensitive. He nipped at it. "You have no idea how good it feels to be here with you. It was difficult convincing myself that national security mattered when I knew I had that key in my pocket."

He waited for a sarcastic comment, but none came. She hadn't said or done anything since he first climbed on top of her. He hiked her leg up a little higher, rubbing their bodies together more fully. Maybe she just needed a little bit more time to wake up.

He brushed his lips back down her throat, the bruises still noticeable even in the semidarkness. She was hurt, a little fragile, he needed to remember that.

"You okay, sweetheart?" He moved the edge of her shirt aside with his lips, kissing across her collarbone. She still didn't answer.

He leaned up on his elbows so he could look down at her more clearly. Her brown eyes stared directly at him. "This can wait, you know." He smiled and trailed a finger across her cheek. He brushed her lips against his and her mouth seemed to automatically open for him. He kissed her again softly. "We can just sleep if you want. Believe it or not, I can convince certain parts of my body to simmer down when needed."

Again, no smart-aleck remark. He didn't even think Lillian was capable of that.

"You're going pretty easy on me tonight," he said. "Are you sure you didn't get some sort of head injury?" He kissed her again. Her lips opened as soon as his touched hers, but then she didn't respond.

As a matter of fact, her hands were still on his shoulders, and hadn't moved. Her leg was still around his hips, where he'd placed it.

As soon as he removed his lips from hers, her mouth closed. Jace bent down to kiss her again and they opened.

But then did nothing.

What the hell was going on?

"Lillian?" He eased his weight off her farther. Her hands remained on his shoulders, her eyes open and looking right at him.

"Lillian." He shook her a little. "Lily? What's going on? Talk to me, sweetheart."

Did she have some sort of head injury he hadn't been aware of? She'd been fine earlier. Maybe a little off her game, stressed, but she certainly hadn't been blanking out when she handled that bomb scare today.

He rolled his weight completely off her. Her arms dropped to her side on the mattress. Her eyes still had that blank stare. Like the body lying here was just an empty shell of the strong, vibrant woman she usually was.

Jace had seen this sort of blank stare before…a checking out of reality. But it had been men in the army suffering from PTSD.

And always, if the person was in no danger of hurting himself or others, the best thing was to leave his subconscious to work through it in his own way.

"Come back to me, Lil. Whatever it is, whatever you're going through, we can work through it."

Tears streamed out of her open eyes and down the sides of her face, but she didn't move, didn't blink, didn't talk.

She was trapped in some hell in her mind and there was nothing Jace could do.

It was only a little over twenty minutes before Lillian came back to him, but it was one of the longest passages of time that he'd ever lived through.

He was still sitting next to her on the bed, holding her hand, when she finally started blinking. Tension rolled through her body and she began breathing more heavily.

"Lily? It's Jace. You're safe."

She snatched her hand out of his before scooting over to the far side of the bed, pulling the comforter up to her chin. Her eyes darted around the room like she was looking for danger. Like she couldn't figure out where she was.

"You're safe, Lillian. You're at a hotel in Denver."

She got out of the bed now, back to the wall, obviously ready to fight.

Jace kept his voice even and his body still, not wanting to send her into a full panic. And he sure as hell didn't want her reaching for the sidearm that sat on the bedside table while she was in this condition. "We're on a mission with the SWAT team to protect the LESS Summit. You...fell asleep. You're disoriented."

It took her a few more moments of him repeating the same words before they began sinking in. And while she didn't relax, at least she didn't look like she was about to fight off an entire army.

"Jace?"

Thank God. "Yeah, sweetheart. It's me. You scared me there for a bit. We were in the middle of making out and I lost you."

To his utter dismay, big tears filled her eyes and rolled down her cheeks. Not counting the tears that had seemed to leak out of her eyes of their own accord a little while ago, this was the first time Jace could remember seeing Lillian cry. The sight of them gutted him.

"Lily—"

She took a step back. "I'm sorry, Jace. Please don't look at me like that. It's not you, it just happens sometimes."

His eyes narrowed. "What happens?"

She squeezed her eyes closed, one hand pulling the blanket more tightly around her, the other gesturing toward the bed. "I blank out during sex. But I promise it's not your fault. It's me. Please don't take it personally. It wasn't you."

Jace could feel bile pooling in his stomach as he took in the ramifications of her words.

This wasn't the first time this had happened to her.

The blackouts didn't have anything to do with combat. This was centered around sex. Steve Drackett had been right back in Ren's office.

Lillian was recovering from some sort of sexual assault.

He forced himself to ignore the way his heart seemed to be shattering around him. He had to understand exactly what she was dealing with. "This happens to you a lot?"

She kept her eyes tightly closed. Almost like a child who believed the monsters would go away if she didn't face them. "I don't want to talk about it. I just didn't want you to think it was your fault. That it was something you did."

He eased a little closer on the bed. "Did it happen this morning when we were together?"

Now her eyes opened. "No! No, this morning was...great. I was there. *Completely* there. The whole time. But this morning was the exception, not the norm."

"But...it happens to you a lot?"

Her tiny nod told him everything he needed to know. The thought of this happening to her when she was with someone else. Someone who wouldn't notice, or worse, take advantage. Jace struggled to tamp down the rage. "*How* often?"

"Until this morning? Pretty much always."

"For how long?" Maybe the trauma was recent. That, while still being horrible, was at least understandable.

She shook her head, obviously not wanting to answer the question. Keeping his hands out in front of him, palms up in a gesture of non-aggression, he eased closer again.

"It's behind me," she whispered. "That's all you need to know."

"It's obviously not behind you, based on the fact that thirty minutes ago when we were kissing, your eyes were open and your hands were on my shoulders, but your conscious mind was miles from that bed. It had hidden itself away to protect your psyche."

She opened her mouth to respond, but no words came out. Finally, she just shook her head.

"You were raped." God, he hated to even say that word to her. It was bitter, unbearable in his mouth.

She nodded, her brown eyes not leaving his.

He thought his heart had already been shattered, but he'd been wrong. Watching that small move of her head confirmed everything he'd feared, but hadn't wanted to believe… The pain nearly doubled him over. "How long ago?"

She shook her head adamantly.

Why would she not want to answer that question? Was it so recent that she couldn't bear to think about it at all?

"Lily, I need you to tell me. I want to be careful not to do or say anything that will trigger you in any way." He got out of the bed and took a step closer, now just a few feet from her, relieved when she didn't flinch away. "What we had this morning was special. It can be again. But I need you to trust me enough to tell me what happened to you so we can navigate this together. Please, baby."

"I can't, Jace," she whispered, those big brown eyes begging him to let it go. "I'm sorry."

He didn't want to push. Didn't want to ask her to give more than she could. But he also couldn't risk doing something that would have her retreating into that shell again.

"Okay, you don't have to talk to me." He pushed down the hurt. This wasn't about him. "But I'm going to go. I don't want to stay here with you and take a chance on triggering you again."

"Jace…"

The pain in her voice tore at him.

"I'm not mad, Tiger Lily." He took a chance and stepped closer. When she didn't move away, he slipped a hand in her hair at the nape of her neck. He pulled her forward until his lips met her forehead. "I understand you don't want to talk about it. But I can't stay here and take a chance on hurting you further. Doing damage because I'm not sure of how to navigate your emotional terrain."

He backed away, giving her the best smile he could. His Lillian was broken, and she didn't trust him enough to try to help her put herself back together. He really wasn't mad about that—she needed to work through this however was best for her. He would be her friend if she wanted it. But he would not take a chance on hurting her further. Of using her the way she'd obviously been used by other men.

"We'll talk more when you're ready. Maybe after this op is over." Pulling away was like a knife ripping him in the gut. But what else could he do? "I just don't want to hurt you more."

He gave her a gentle nod, then turned and walked toward the door. He was almost to it, hand on the knob, when he heard her words. He'd thought nothing she could say would've been worse than the initial knowledge that she'd been raped.

He was so, so wrong.

Her words changed everything he'd always held true.

"Twelve. I was raped twelve years ago."

Chapter Fifteen

What was she doing? Was she really going to tell Jace the truth? The truth about her? About Daryl? About what had really happened?

She'd only ever spoken about it to Grace Parker. And even then she'd left out details. Jace was not going to let her leave out details.

He turned from the door and moved back into the main section of the room. She could see his blue eyes staring out at her. Not in disbelief—she'd never for one second thought he wouldn't believe her—but in full tactical mode.

He was trying to put together the pieces.

"Lil, you have to just tell me. Because I swear nothing you could say would be any worse than what I'm imagining in my mind."

Wanna bet?

She didn't say the words but knew the truth was worse than whatever Jace was thinking. Was almost more than she could bear to think about. She didn't want to hurt him unnecessarily. Daryl was his brother. They'd never gotten along, and Jace had joined the army to get out from Daryl's thumb as soon as possible, but Daryl had been his brother.

No one would want to believe their own flesh and blood was capable of what his brother had done.

"Oh, God, it was Daryl, wasn't it?"

The anguish in Jace's voice made her want to rush to him, to hold him. To erase the agony in his eyes as she nodded.

He seemed to age right before her eyes. "Tell me."

"It was after my eighteenth birthday. The day before we were supposed to leave. After you and I…" She nodded and shrugged.

Jace knew what she meant. After they'd had sex. She'd wanted to have sex with him for months before her birthday, but he'd refused everything but making out. Had said they'd have a lifetime together to make love. They could at least wait until they were both legal.

God, she'd loved him for that. It had made her feel so special, cherished. That she was worth waiting for.

"I got a text from you saying to meet you at the warehouse," she continued. Daryl's warehouse, where a lot of his illegal activities had taken place. "I knew you didn't like me to go there alone, but I thought you'd gotten home from your job for Daryl early. The last job. I can't even remember what it was anymore." Not surprising, given all that had happened afterward.

"I was supposed to deliver an order of pharmaceutical drugs," Jace whispered. "To a place clear on the other side of the state. The dealer I was supposed to deliver them to never even showed up."

They looked at each other, realizing now it had all been a setup.

Lillian moved back over to the window, needing some distance, unable to face the blueness of Jace's eyes for this next part. "I got to the warehouse and Daryl was waiting for me. Said he had found out we were leaving to join the army. Said there was no way he was going to let two of his best and most loyal runners leave at the same time."

God, she'd been so naive. Had thought there was nothing Daryl could do to stop them. Had laughed at Daryl and told him that. Now that she was eighteen she could go wherever she wanted. And Jace had already been twenty. He would've left earlier if it hadn't been for her. If he hadn't wanted to be able to leave with her legally.

She wished they'd just run away from the very beginning.

"I told him he couldn't stop us, we were leaving the next day." She pressed her head against the cold glass. "He hit me in the stomach over and over. Dislocated my shoulder. Kicked me in the legs. It was before I knew how to fight. How to protect myself."

The muscles and bones in question still twinged in horrific memory.

"He didn't hit you in the face."

She could hear the coarse tightness in Jace's voice.

She shook her head against the glass. "No," she whispered.

"Because he didn't want there to be any bruises I could see. He knew that if I thought he'd forced you in any way, I would fight him. Kill him."

She heard Jace pacing.

"Or die trying to get you out."

"He—he raped me. Then locked me in the tiny janitor's closet and left me in there all night. I knew you'd be looking for me. That all I had to do was survive until you found me." That whole day was a blur of pain and trauma, but *that* she could remember. The knowledge that Jace would come for her. Would make her world all right again.

"Lillian…"

The pain in his voice was too much. She continued faster. She wasn't helping either of them by dragging it out like this. She took a second to distance herself from the story mentally. "Daryl came back and got me the next morning. I was in pretty bad shape from the beating. He raped me again, then threw clean clothes at me to put on. Told me to get dressed, that you were coming over."

She heard Jace's strangled sound behind her. She continued. "Daryl told me there was no way both of us were leaving. He told me he had one of the guys in the rafters of the warehouse, with a rifle on you. Told me that if I didn't just sit there and shut up, he would have you shot. And that while you were bleeding out he would rape me again right in front of you before you died."

Jace's curse was vile.

She finally turned from the window. "Looking back on it now, I think he was bluffing. You were his *brother*. I don't think he would've killed you. He might have killed me to keep you from leaving, but he wasn't going to kill you."

"Lily…" He took a step toward her, but she held out a hand to ward him off. He could not touch her right now. Not at this very second.

"Daryl overplayed his hand. I think he thought

you would come back. That you would fight him for me or something. I'm not sure. I don't think either of us thought you would just believe his lies so easily. Believe that I just jumped into his bed straight from yours."

Jace shook his head, no color left in his face. "Daryl came to see me a couple hours before I came by there. Told me you had come to him. That you had said I was moving too fast, that you didn't want to leave. That you didn't know how to tell me you weren't coming with me to join the army. That you wanted his protection and were even willing to sleep with him if that was what it cost."

She hadn't known any of that. "You believed him?"

"No, although I had to admit it was not outside the realm of possibility. I was talking forever and marriage and you were barely eighteen, for crying out loud. Thinking I was pushing too hard was my button. And Daryl didn't just push it, he *stomped* on it."

"It was always his talent."

"When I got to the warehouse and saw you there, saw you clinging to him… I thought for once in his miserable life my brother was telling the truth. That I had pushed you too hard."

She nodded. "He manipulated us both."

"I'm so sorry, Lily. I should've gotten you alone. Talked to you."

She shook her head. "I wouldn't have told you. I really thought he would kill you."

"Why didn't you come find me afterward? Once I was in the army Daryl couldn't hurt me."

She'd told him this much. She had to tell it all. "He kept me locked up. In that closet. He knew I would run, would tell you if I got the chance. He kept me there in the dark and only let me out when he…when he…"

She didn't finish, but she didn't have to. Jace knew what she meant. Daryl let her out when he raped her. Those days, those weeks, were all a blur of agony and darkness to her. When Daryl had gotten tired of her, he'd given her to a couple of his best men as a reward.

By then her brain had learned to check out every time a man touched her. So she didn't remember that at all.

"He had other girls there, Jace. Daryl did. I think it's part of the reason both of us were feeling the itch to get out. It was one thing to run drugs or weapons every once in a while…"

"Quite another to find out human trafficking is involved," he said, finishing for her, and nodding. "I had my suspicions things might be heading that way before I left, but didn't have any proof. And then Daryl died and everything he'd put together disbanded, so there wasn't much point in trying to prove it one way or another."

She had to tell him all of it, Lillian knew that. Would he hate her for it? It didn't matter, because even if he did, she didn't regret her actions. "I killed him, Jace."

He didn't even blink. "Good."

"I'm serious. I was…with him when the fire started. He ran over to see what was happening and I hit him over the head with a bottle of tequila he had lying around. The whole building was going up in flames and I ran."

"Good," Jace said again.

"You don't understand, I could've told someone Daryl was still in there. There probably would've been time to get him out."

"No, you don't understand, Lily. I'm glad you killed him. That saves me the trouble of committing cold-blooded murder now. Because that's exactly what would be happening if my bastard brother was still alive."

Relief coursed through Lillian.

"You look surprised." He shook his head. "Did you really think I would be okay with what Daryl did to you?"

She shrugged. "He was your brother."

"He stopped being my brother twelve years

ago, the second he touched you. Don't have any doubt about that." He scrubbed his hands across his face, looking older. Pained. "I can never make up for what happened to you. But I am so sorry."

"It wasn't your fault."

She flinched as Jace slammed the back of his fist against the wall. "It damn well was my fault. At least part of it. I knew Daryl was edging from risky ventures into downright dangerous ones. Knew he was crossing lines that no one would think was okay."

"That's why you wanted out."

He took a step toward her. "That's why I wanted *both* of us out. Because he was becoming unstable. It was just a matter of time before everything blew up in his face—which it did, literally—and I didn't want us caught in the flames."

They stared at each other for long minutes.

"Why did you believe him, Jace?" Why hadn't he been able to see the truth?

"It's like you said, Daryl was the master manipulator. He'd played on my deepest fear, that I really was rushing you. You were so young. Hadn't had any life experiences. That I was forcing you into a life you didn't really want, taking away your choices."

"I wanted to go," she whispered. More than

anything in the world she'd wanted to leave with Jace.

"I was a fool. Blinded to the truth by my own insecurities. That you might want someone like Daryl. More powerful. Stronger. He hinted that it was true and I bought it like a sale at Christmas."

Her heart broke as she watched his eyes fill up with tears.

"I'll never forgive myself, Lily."

"You didn't know."

"I should've reconfirmed. I should've made sure you were okay. Hell, even if you really did want him, I should've barged in and tried to convince you otherwise. The first thing we learn in the army is that you never leave someone behind. I left you behind, Lil. You were tortured, for God's sake."

She wanted to disagree with him but knew words wouldn't pacify him. And he was right. She had been tortured. Physically, mentally, emotionally.

She couldn't take his pain away, but she could help him understand what had come from it. The phoenix that had risen from the ashes. "But I grew stronger, Jace. Yeah, I may still be a bit of a mess when it comes to sex." He flinched, but she continued. "But I'm also a kick-ass warrior because of what Daryl did to me. I became determined never to be a victim again. And have spent my life trying to keep other people from being victims also."

"You *are* a warrior, Lil. A formidable one."

She felt something ease in her heart. "I am. I know that. And because of it—knowing the lives I've saved in the years since I've joined Omega—I can't fully regret what happened to me."

"The blackouts…"

Now it was her turn to rub a hand across her face. "The blackouts are problematic. And part of it was because I refused to get emotionally attached to anyone before having sex with him. I was working with a psychiatrist about that before she…died. But I didn't have a blackout with you this morning, Jace. I was with you. Completely focused on the moment. And it was the best thing that has happened to me in a dozen years. My body remembers you, I think. Or my mind knows that you would never hurt me."

He took a step toward her. "I would never hurt you, Lil. Never."

She smiled. "I know. I've always known. And even with my blackouts… I'm not afraid. I'm confident of my ability to fight my way out of any situation if needed. But it's like my brain doesn't know how to process the old and the new information together. I feel a man's weight on me and my brain just shuts down."

"And when you come back?"

"I have no memory of what has happened. My brain is still trying to protect me from trauma even all these years later. Even though I don't want it to. Grace—my psychiatrist before that bastard Damien Freihof killed her—said it was because those men meant nothing to me. That eventually when I had sex with someone who I truly cared about, my brain wouldn't shut down."

"Like this morning." The ghost of a smile crossed his lips but then disappeared. "How can you ever forgive me? How can you even bear to be in the same room as me? I failed you so completely."

She walked over to him, more confidence filling her with every step. Grace had been right. Her brain had been shutting down because she was making bad choices, not because of fear. Now that she had the chance to be with someone she knew cared about her, she wasn't going to shut down.

"Jace, you would never have left me there if you'd known." She cupped his cheeks. "I always knew that. You would've died trying to get me out. We both made mistakes. We both paid a price. But I refuse to give Daryl any more of my history. He's dead. He can stay dead."

"You blanked on me tonight."

She shrugged. "I'm always going to have triggers. Maybe just make sure I'm always fully awake before starting anything."

"Deal. As long as you promise to tell me if anything I do or say starts to frighten you in any way."

She breathed a silent sigh of relief when he wrapped his arms around her. She listened to the reassuring beat of his heart for long minutes. "I was afraid you wouldn't want me once you knew."

"Not wanting you is never even going to be an option, Tiger Lily."

"Good, because I'd like to give tonight another try. I hate to think I'd missed out on all the fun."

"Are you sure? We can just sleep. We don't have to—"

She kissed him. She knew he was feeling guilty. But if there was one thing her training had taught her, it was that facing problems head-on as soon as they came along meant that they didn't grow into something insurmountable the next day.

Like she said, she refused to give up any more ground to Daryl Eakin. He'd taken too much. Now he could stay in his grave, where he belonged.

The brother she was always supposed to be with was here in her arms. She pressed herself closer to him, deepening the kiss. When she heard him groan, she knew she had him.

And this time she wasn't sure she was ever going to be able to let him go.

Chapter Sixteen

Four hours later, Jace was out for a run, push-ing himself much harder than he should have, given the parameters of the mission and what would be required of him over the next two days. Lillian had reported back for her shift about thirty minutes ago.

He turned down Oak, a deserted street, glad the temperature was at least a little over freez-ing even though it was February, and he didn't have to worry about ice. He knew enough about Denver to know he was on the rougher side of town, but he wished—Jace literally looked up at a star in the night sky and *wished*—some asshole would mess with him right now.

Jace wanted to fight. To feel the bones of some predator breaking under his hands. To throw his head back and howl in agony.

But mostly he wanted to go back in time and change what had happened to Lillian.

Daryl.

Jace wasn't kidding when he said it was a good thing his brother was dead. Otherwise Jace couldn't promise he wouldn't be about to turn his back on everything he'd ever held important and true—law, order, justice—and be on his way to kill his brother right at this second.

He was glad Lillian had left the bastard there in that fire. Had saved herself.

Jace had been in boot camp when Daryl died. The body had already been identified by one of Daryl's friends and put in a closed casket by the time Jace arrived, so Jace didn't know if Daryl had suffered, had burned. He'd hoped not, at the time. But now that had changed.

He took a turn down another deserted street, relishing the feel of the colder wind as it blew between buildings, the ache of his muscles as he pushed them further, the tightness of his lungs as he tried to draw in air.

Jace wasn't sure he was ever going to be able to draw in a full breath again for the rest of his life without it hurting.

He had failed Lillian in the worst way someone could fail another. The thought of her helpless in Daryl's clutches for two weeks burned like acid in his gut. She'd been so young, maybe not exactly helpless, but nowhere near the warrior she was now.

She'd been raped and abused so many times that her mind had shut down almost every time she'd tried to have sex since then.

And Jace…well, he'd just happily lived with his self-proclaimed righteous anger for a dozen years, believing *he'd* been the one who'd been wronged.

It would be downright laughable if it wasn't so pathetic.

The miracle of it all was that Lily didn't hate him. He'd watched her as she'd slept after their lovemaking tonight.

Lovemaking that had taken on an entirely new tenor. Now that Jace knew how close he'd come to losing her—physically, emotionally, in every way possible—all he could do was cherish her. Worship her with his body.

She hadn't let him treat her like she was fragile. And he did understand that. Lillian wasn't fragile.

But damn if he wouldn't treat her like the treasure she was. The treasure he would've had next to him, healthy and whole, for the past twelve years if he hadn't been so blinded by his own insecurities and tricked by a psychopath's words.

So many mistakes.

Watching Lily as she slept, he'd tried to process everything. Tried to wrap his head around the enormity of it all. He'd refused to let rage consume him at that moment. All he wanted to do was be there for her. Hold her if she needed it. Pull her back if she began to slip away again.

But she hadn't. She'd stayed there with him—with them—the entire time. No scary blank stares and waking up not knowing where she was. He'd counted every single second with her as a treasure.

When she'd gotten up and dressed to head in for her SWAT shift, he'd just watched her. Leaned back in the bed with his arm tucked behind his head, and stared at her as if he didn't have anywhere else in the world he'd rather be.

Which was damn near the truth.

"Pretty sexy, huh?" She'd gestured to her cargo pants and tactical boots.

"Damn right, more sexy on you than me."

She grinned at him, waggling her eyebrows. "I'm not so sure about that."

In that moment, grinning at each other, just enjoying each other's company the way they always had, it was impossible to reconcile that this woman—so in control, capable, strong—had been damaged in such a way.

He'd fought to not let his smile slip. Refused to look at her with concern or sympathy in his eyes. That wasn't what Lillian needed. The phoenix had risen from the ashes on her own.

He would not drag her back down as he came to grips.

But now as he was out running, away from her, the rage coursed through him. Jace let it. Let his muscles take the punishment as his mind struggled to comprehend everything. By the time he made it back to the hotel, he was dripping with sweat, despite the cold. He wiped himself down with his sweatshirt before entering the lobby. Even though it wasn't time for his shift, he'd grab breakfast and head back to city hall.

Because sleep was not in the cards for Jace any time soon. It would be a long time before he could close his eyes and not picture an eighteen-year-old Lillian hurt, terrified, hoping he was going to rescue her from the darkness.

A rescue that had never occurred.

Rage pooled through him again.

"Eakin, are we not giving you enough to do that you need to spend your downtime doing extra workouts?" Derek was getting a cup of coffee from the small breakfast section of the hotel.

Jace couldn't even smile at the other man. "Just needed to work off some steam. Trust me, this will help me be more focused."

"You look like you'd like to go ten rounds

with someone in the ring. This have anything to do with a petite brunette we both know?"

"She's not the one I want to fight, believe it or not. Although I'm sure she'd give me a run for my money anyway."

Derek offered Jace a glass of water from his table while he continued to sip his coffee. Jace thanked him with a tip of his head while he drank it down. The two of them studied each other in silence for a long moment.

"Is this where you warn me not to hurt her? To keep away from her?" Jace knew his tone was combative. Left over from his own frustrations.

Derek, unflappable as ever, just smiled and shook his head. "Lillian can take care of herself. If you hurt her, she'll be the one to kick your ass. I won't have to do it. To be honest, I'm just glad she's letting someone close enough to even be in the realm of possibility of hurting her."

"Maybe she has her reasons for not letting people close."

"Maybe." Derek held his hands out in a motion of surrender. "I'm not trying to fight with you, Jace. I've been her team leader, and *friend*, long enough to know that Lillian has some scars. And I'm human enough to know that not all scars are visible."

All the frustration just flowed out of Jace, despair taking its place. "Scars I could've prevented."

Derek pushed out the chair across from him with his foot and gestured for Jace to sit in it. "My wife is a forensic scientist. Works part-time for Omega now that we have a baby at home. Molly is quite possibly the most opposite of Lillian possible."

"How so?"

"Molly is shy, quiet, insecure outside the lab. She couldn't do a pull-up to save her life, and despite my best effort to teach her otherwise, still punches with her thumb resting against the side of her fist."

That caused the slightest of smiles to break out on his face. "Like a girl."

Derek's smile was much bigger. "Exactly."

"Lillian doesn't punch like a girl."

"No, she very definitely does not. Molly is soft. And I mean that in the very best way that word can be used. And we both know that Lillian is not soft. And I mean that also in the very best way."

Jace knew Derek had a point, so he took a sip of water while he waited for him to continue.

"A couple of years ago a psychopath kidnapped my Molly." All hint of a smile was gone from Derek now. "Drugged and tortured her. Got her a second time and began breaking her fingers one by one while he was on the phone with me."

Jace sat up straighter. "Damn."

"What would Lillian do if someone did that to her?"

"I don't know. Probably work out a dozen different moves so that it would never happen again."

"Exactly. That's *exactly* what Lillian would do. Because Lillian needs to know that she can take care of herself physically in whatever situation she finds herself in. That under normal circumstances—Tasers being the exception—no one will ever get the drop on her again. Something she learned the hardest of ways before I ever met her."

Jace could only nod.

"Lillian and Molly are different because I've tried to teach Molly some self-defense moves, and while she'll learn them to humor me, generally after twenty minutes of practice she leans over and whispers that she'll just trust me to come rescue her if she ever gets back in another dangerous situation." Derek grinned. "Then distracts me into activities not having anything to do with self-defense."

"Somehow I can't imagine Lillian ever doing that."

"Of course not. But mostly because Lillian

is never going to need you to come rescue her from a dangerous situation."

"Because in almost all situations she can rescue herself." Jace leaned back in his chair. "It's not that I don't appreciate it, but I'm not sure I'm getting the main point of your little pep talk."

"My point is, I never mistake Molly's softness for weakness. And her trust that I will get to her no matter what if she needs me is a vow I take very seriously. I will save her or die trying. But the fact is, Molly also saved me. Her strength—her emotional fortitude—is what dragged me out of the darkness when I couldn't find the way myself."

Jace nodded.

"Now, my wife is brilliant," Derek continued after another sip from his cup of coffee. "So she never asked me if I needed any emotional self-defense lessons. Not that she had to be brilliant to figure out that I'm too stubborn to admit I might need help in that department. But the fact of the matter is this—the same way she trusts that I'll get her out if she's in trouble physically, I know she'll get me out if I'm in trouble emotionally."

"And you think that's what Lillian needs."

"I think she can take care of herself physically, but emotionally is a different story. She won't ever ask for help. Hell, I don't even know if she knows *how* to ask for it. I sure as hell didn't with Molly."

Derek was right. Probably about all of it.

"And believe it or not, helping her in that way—helping her discover and meet her emotional needs—is going to help you just as much as it helps her. I'm going to assume that whatever has you running like the hounds of hell are chasing you in the middle of a February night has to do with Lillian's scars."

"Maybe."

"Well, running or fighting or smashing your fist against a wall may help you feel better temporarily, but ultimately it's going to be helping Lillian heal in the way she needs most that's going to make this rage pass."

"Derek, I'm not sure this rage is ever going to pass."

"Maybe not. But she doesn't need your rage. Lillian's got enough of that herself. She doesn't need you to fight her physical battles for her, but she needs you to stand with her emotionally. Of course, if you're just around temporarily, then maybe you shouldn't even try to get close to her."

"That's not the issue. I've owned a ranch outside Colorado Springs for a number of years now. Have plans to raise animals."

"Like what you were talking about with that bridge jumper?"

"Exactly. Someplace people could go who have PTSD, who just need to get away."

"It's interesting that the two of you lost touch with each other so long ago and then ultimately ended up settling within fifty miles of each other."

That fact had not escaped Jace's attention, either. He nodded. But he also knew that physical proximity wasn't enough. "I just hope she'll give me the chance." Because despite the great sex and friendly banter between them, Jace wasn't sure Lillian would be able to ever truly give herself to a man again.

Especially not him.

Chapter Seventeen

Dawn on the day of the summit found the streets of Denver packed with people of every type: angry, happy, scared.

And they were all loud and carrying signs.

The cold front that had settled over Denver this morning hadn't seemed to deter people. Nobody had expected this many this early, and while the Denver PD were in charge of crowd control, and so far doing a good job of it, Lillian had found she had to fight her way just to get from the hotel back to the City and County Building.

It was going to be a long day. The entire team would be on high alert as the politicians, police chiefs and other high-profile shareholders in the LESS program from all over the country arrived. The official debut and demonstration was scheduled for six hours from now.

Jace was already on-site, the rest of the team either already there or, like Lillian, on their way. She and Jace hadn't had much more time off together, but just having him near, knowing the truth was finally out between them, had eased a heaviness in Lillian that, along with the weight of everything else, she hadn't even known she'd been carrying.

Jace had never stopped looking with anything less than respect in his eyes. No pity. No sideways glances to make sure she wasn't about to fall apart. Just respect.

And lust. She'd take both.

But not right now. Today there was no room for anything else but the LESS Summit.

Derek was coordinating with the transportation security team of the summit members. Once they were released from the vehicles in the underground parking garage and escorted into the building, the summit members would officially be Omega Sector's responsibility.

As Lillian elbowed her way past another set of protestors, she couldn't shake the feeling in her gut.

Trouble. The air was all but saturated with it.

Lillian wasn't prone to superstition or gut feelings. She liked to make informed decisions based on facts and preparation.

But she couldn't get the hairs on the back of her neck to settle down. Someone was here with death on their mind.

It didn't take a genius to guess that person was Damien Freihof. This was a perfect stage for him to continue his sick play. But they had spent the last day and a half making sure security was as tight as it possibly could be inside city hall.

She ducked as a protestor haphazardly thrust a sign in her direction, her feeling of dread increasing. What if Freihof's plan wasn't to destroy the summit itself, but to attack the people out here? Nobody was guarding them.

Freihof had never gone after innocent people. He'd focused his attacks over the past few months on people attached to Omega Sector. Their loved ones. But that didn't mean he wouldn't change his MO. And ultimately they couldn't protect everyone in the world from him. But they would damn well make sure city hall and the summit were secure.

Lillian finally forced her way through the crowd and into the building. She identified herself to the security officers. She was about to head to the third floor—to the auditorium where the summit would be held—when she caught sight of someone slipping through the door leading down to the basement. The same one where she'd almost died.

And if she wasn't mistaken, it was Philip Carnell heading down there. Philip, who should be up in the control room right now, finalizing details. Lillian could think of a number of reasons why Carnell might be heading down to the basement level, and none of them were good.

She'd stayed away from Carnell over the last day, since she'd accused him of being the mole. Both Jace and Derek had been watching him and assured her they didn't think Carnell was the traitor. That he hadn't made any suspicious moves.

This was damn well suspicious.

She reached for her comm unit, then cursed when she remembered she hadn't checked in yet, so she didn't have it. She jogged over to the corner door Carnell had disappeared through. She didn't want to go barreling in, accusing him once again of malicious intent—that was probably the surest way to get herself on administrative leave. But she wasn't going to just let him get away with whatever he was doing. If Carnell was moving to assist Freihof in some way, she was going to stop him. And she'd text Jace or Derek once she knew what was going on.

She opened the stairwell door quietly, closing it behind her gently so it didn't make a click. The subbasement was three floors below the lobby level and she could hear Carnell's steps as he moved quickly down the stairs.

Lillian followed silently, listening for the door she knew would lead to the basement. When the sound didn't come she moved more quickly, trying to figure out what was going on. When she got to the door, she stopped, staring at it.

It was closed. Locked with a bolt and padlock Omega had put there to keep this entire basement floor unavailable for the summit. There was no way Carnell just opened this door and went through it without her hearing. She spun around, but Carnell was nowhere to be found and there was nowhere to hide. The only other room was a small closet at the end of the hall. She'd seen it herself yesterday while double-checking the security of this level.

If Carnell was in there, he was hiding, because there was nowhere else to go.

Maybe waiting with his handy Taser? Not this time, rat bastard.

She pulled out her extendable sentry baton from its holder at the back of her belt. With a flick of her wrist it was open to its full length of over eighteen inches. A Taser wasn't going to help Carnell this time.

Deciding the element of surprise was her best bet, Lillian threw open the closet door, then jumped back, expecting to see Carnell pounce toward her. When nothing happened, she grabbed her flashlight and shined it into the closet, baton still raised.

Empty. Cleaning supplies, shelves, but no Carnell.

What the hell?

There was nowhere else he could've gone. She'd come through the lobby level, and the subbasement level was still locked. So where the hell had Carnell gone?

She was turning to backtrack, to see what she'd missed, when she felt it. Just the slightest of breezes. But it was coming from the closet behind her, not the hallway.

How could a breeze be coming from a closet?

Lillian spun her flashlight back around, looking more carefully at the walls of the closet. One of the shelving units was ajar, not flush against the wall. Putting her baton back in the holder, she stepped closer and aimed her flashlight more fully at the gap between the wall and shelf.

It was an opening of some kind.

Knowing Carnell could already be into the deadly stages of whatever he had planned, Lillian didn't hesitate. She flipped off her light and slid the shelf just the smallest amount needed for her to fit through.

She stayed low and alert, allowing her eyes to adjust to the darkened space, expecting another basement room. It was more. A series of rooms, interconnected with a number of doors.

What was this place? The damp, darkened cinder blocks suggested this had been built decades ago, if not longer. Definitely not recently.

But these rooms should've been in the building plans. Even if the rooms weren't being used, the information about them should've been made available.

She had to call this in. There was no way in hell Carnell could accuse her of acting unreasonably now by following and accusing him of misconduct. City hall was not secure.

Her phone was in her hand when she saw Carnell come running out of one room—a look of frustration and concern clear on his face—before turning and opening another door. What the hell was he doing?

She couldn't lose him now. Lillian slipped her phone back in the pocket of her tactical vest and, keeping to the edge of the wall and shadows as much as possible, moved toward the door Carnell had just entered.

She opened the door and found Carnell with his back to her, kneeling on the floor.

Facing the largest explosive device she'd ever seen. That thing would bring down the entire building and everyone in it.

Lillian pulled her weapon out. "Step away

from the device, Carnell. Do it right now. Get
your hands up."

"Muir, listen…"

"Right damn now, Carnell." Lillian took another step closer.

Carnell raised his hands. "It's not what you
think."

She let out a curse with her laugh. "Really?
Because what I think is that I am looking at
you messing with a big-ass bomb. Is that not
the case?"

Lillian felt the movement behind her just a
second too late. A gun was resting at her temple before she could make a move.

"I think what dear Philip is trying to tell you
is that it's not *his* big-ass bomb, isn't that right,
Phil?"

Saul Poniard.

"What the hell are you doing, Saul? Are you
guys working together?"

Saul gave her that friendly smile she now re-
alized had always been completely fake. "Nah.
Not working together. Phil must've stumbled
onto my contribution to the LESS Summit."
He pressed the gun deeper against her temple.
"Gun on the floor, Muir."

Lillian gritted her teeth and placed her Glock
on the floor. She would be able to take him in a
fight, but there was no way she could stop him

from shooting her with his gun at point-blank range. He immediately kicked it away.

"Did you position yourself on my weak side on purpose, Saul, or did you just get lucky?"

Saul shot her a grin. "What can I say, Lily? You taught me well."

"I also taught you not to call me Lily."

"Eakin gets to, so why can't I?"

"Maybe because Jace isn't a lying, traitorous psychopath who plans to blow up a bunch of innocent people."

Saul actually chuckled. "Don't be so shortsighted, *Lily*. I plan to do much more than just blow up the people here."

"Oh, my God, those things are real?" Philip, still standing over by the explosive device, sounded like he was going to vomit.

"Shut up, Phil. It's not quite time to reveal the whole plan. Get down on your knees, hands behind your head."

He gave Lillian a shove toward the floor. Reining in her temper, she dropped to her knees. A time to fight was coming, but she needed to wait until she had some sort of a chance. If Jace was here, he'd do something to distract Saul long enough for her to be able to move on him.

Philip Carnell just looked like he might pee his pants. No help was coming from him.

And if she tried anything on her own right now, she'd just get a bullet in the brain for her troubles. But when Saul secured her wrists behind her back with a zip tie, she wished she had tried.

"Saul," she said, "you have to know that Derek's going to notice that we're missing. Maybe you not being around would've been overlooked, but all three of us not being at our proper places? They'll never hold the summit here. They'll cancel it outright."

"That's why you're going to call your boyfriend and tell him you found proof that Phil is the mole, that you've got him in custody and you'll be reporting soon. I'm sure in all the chaos and relief that they finally caught the person giving information to Freihof, they won't even notice I'm missing."

Lillian just shook her head at him. "You know I won't do it, Poniard. You can go to hell."

The friendly surfer facade disappeared from his face. Saul grabbed her by the hair and snatched her head back. He pointed the gun at her temple again. "I think you will."

"You're going to kill me anyway. We both know that. So why would I help you blow up a building full of innocent people? Not to mention all the protestors outside that would also get hurt in the panic."

He gripped her hair harder and jerked her head to the side, pulling out a knife from his own SWAT vest. "I think you will, Muir."

Lillian didn't even try to stop the laugh that bubbled out of her. "You think you can torture me into helping you? You're the one on the clock, Saul. Every second we spend down here is another second the team continues to wonder where we are. Just a matter of time before they empty the building. I daresay I can withstand any torture you want to dish out until they do that."

Damn it, she didn't want to die. Not now… right when she was beginning to find herself again. And Jace. Not when there was the possibility of a wonderful new beginning.

But she would. She would take whatever Saul thought he could do to her to get her to lie to the team.

She saw his fist flying toward her face but couldn't brace herself with her hands tied behind her back. She fell to the floor hard, but forced herself to sit back up immediately.

She spat blood to the side of Saul's feet. "You're going to have to do better than that."

She expected his fist again, or a kick. But instead Saul just laughed. "Actually, you're right. Nobody could ever break you physically in that short amount of time. But I don't have to break you." He turned to Philip. "I'll break *him*."

Saul began walking toward Philip, who had stayed silent during their exchange. Before she could say anything to stop him, Saul did a one-two combination move, punching Philip in the abdomen, followed by a roundhouse kick to the jaw.

Philip fell to the floor, groaning.

Saul turned and actually winked at Lillian. How had she ever found him likable? "You helped me perfect that move. Thanks."

She watched in horror as he turned back to Philip and stabbed him in the shoulder, ripped out the blade, then brought it back down and sliced through Philip's arm. Philip's anguished cry tore at her heart.

"Damn it, Saul…"

"One call, Lillian. Just two sentences."

Philip shook his head back and forth. "No, Lillian, you can't."

Saul sliced at Philip again. Saul was trained in combat. Philip's fighting ability was minimal at best, and without a weapon, he was a sitting duck.

"Enough, Poniard," Lillian yelled. She had to get Saul's attention back on her.

"I don't have time for this. So you either make the call or the next stab is into a vital organ of Phil's. Then, if you still won't do it, I'm going outside, grabbing the first mom and kid I find and bringing them down here. We'll see how long they can withstand torture."

"Lillian…" Philip's words came out between jagged breaths. "He's bluffing. Don't…"

Saul brought the knife back up and she knew he meant what he'd said.

And knew what she had to do.

"Stop!" she yelled. "I'll do it."

Saul snickered at her but at least walked away from Philip, who was still lying on the floor groaning, blood spilling from his wounds.

Saul got right into Lillian's face. The temptation to head-butt him was overwhelming, but she knew it wouldn't accomplish anything.

"You know what your problem is, Lily? Lack of follow-through. You can't stand to see others get hurt, even when it's necessary for change. Surely you can see that we've reached a point where change is necessary in modern law enforcement?"

"The only thing necessary for me is for you to stop monologuing. Give me the damn phone."

He pulled out her phone, along with his Glock, and after punching Jace's contact button, put the gun to one of her ears and the phone to the other. "Talk to the boyfriend and tell him you've got Philip in custody and have proof he's the mole. That you'll be back as soon as you can." He tapped the side of her head with the gun. "You try to tell him what's really going on and I will make sure you see innocent people die right in front of you as horrifically as possible. They'll die screaming."

Lillian pursed her lips. "All right, simmer down there, Hulk-Smash. Give me the goddamn phone."

Saul hit the send button for Jace.

"Hey, you."

Just hearing his deep voice helped settle her. Like it always had.

"Hey." Her own voice came out husky.

"Where are you? Derek was expecting you nearly thirty minutes ago."

Saul narrowed his eyes at her and brought his knife up in Philip's direction.

"Jace, tell Derek it's going to be a while before I make it in. Don't be mad, but I caught Carnell sneaking into the marked-off basement and I followed him. I caught him, Jace. Have him in custody. I'll explain later, but Carnell is definitely the mole."

"You're sure?"

She had to find a way to warn Jace. She hoped this worked. "One-hundred-percent. I swear on my brother's life I'm telling the truth."

Jace laughed. "You don't have a brother."

Lillian gave the most lighthearted chuckle she was capable of. "Fine. Then I swear on your brother's life that I'm telling the truth. You know how much I love your dear brother."

"Yeah, a lot of love." The slightest change in Jace's tone clued her in. He knew there was something up. She had his attention now. "You need help bringing in Philip? There's nothing going on around here until the bigwigs arrive."

Saul shook his head in warning.

"Nah. I can definitely handle Carnell. You stay where you are. He won't get the drop on me down here again."

Would Jace understand? It was all so vague.

"You sure?"

"If Philip keeps running his mouth, he's going to end up just like that perp Daryl. You remember me telling you about what I did to Daryl?" She chuckled again to try to throw Saul off. "Carnell is going to end up just like him if he keeps talking trash to me."

"Hey, you be good," Jace finally said. "And be careful. Don't want you to get in any trouble for roughing up a suspect."

"I'll see you in a bit."

Saul hit the disconnect button as soon as the last word was out of her mouth. She could only pray Jace understood what she was trying to tell him.

"Who the hell is Daryl?" Saul hissed. "Why'd you bring him up?"

"He's just some guy I fought with once. And I brought him up because if I treat Jace like we're nothing more than professional colleagues, he's going to know something's up, okay? You got what you wanted, Saul, you damn coward, so just shut the hell up."

She saw his face turn red with rage, as his arm flew toward her. The world spun to black as he cracked her in the back of the head with the butt of his gun.

Chapter Eighteen

The second Lillian's call disconnected, Jace was running out into the hallway to find Derek.

"We need to evacuate the building right now."

Derek immediately put away the papers he was looking at. "Why? What happened?"

"I just talked to Lillian. She's in trouble. And there's a bomb in the building, probably in the basement."

"She told you that? Why didn't she radio it in? Call the bomb squad?"

"She was talking to me under duress, trying to get me a message. She was talking about my brother, Daryl."

Derek looked confused. "Your brother, Daryl, planted a bomb?"

"No, my brother, Daryl, is dead. But he died in an explosion. Lillian was trying to get that across to me by mentioning him."

Derek shook his head. "No offense, Eakin,

but are you sure? Maybe she was just bringing him up as part of a conversation."

Jace stepped farther into Derek's personal space. They didn't have time to waste. "She told me she had proof that Philip Carnell was the mole. That she caught him. That she would swear on her brother's life that it was him."

"I didn't know Lillian had a brother."

"She doesn't. When I brought up that point, she said she would swear on *my* brother's life that Carnell was the mole."

"Okay, weird. But what makes you think she's under duress?"

Without providing details about Daryl that Lillian might not want to share, Jace explained what she had said about Daryl and what she was trying to explain to them.

Jace knew without a shadow of a doubt that Lillian had risked her life to get him that message. He wasn't going to waste what she'd done, regardless of whether Derek agreed or not. He didn't want to have to go over Derek's head, but he would if he had to.

Jace trusted Lillian. Trusted what she was trying to tell him. He couldn't even allow himself to think about the fact that she had now served her purpose for whoever had forced her to make that call and might already be dead. Because that damn well wasn't going to happen.

"Derek, I'm right. You know Lillian would've handled this differently if Carnell really was in custody. She wouldn't just leave us in the middle of an important lockdown when every person on the team is needed. Not to mention, she would've died before calling and leading us astray unless she had a plan to try to warn us. *Mentioning Daryl was that plan*."

"All right, I trust you. And moreover, I trust Lillian. Let's get this building cleared now. But calmly."

Within seconds Derek was on the comm units with the rest of the Omega team and the added security personnel. Thankfully, because of the LESS Summit, half the people who would normally be working here had been given the day off. Within minutes everyone with security clearance was helping to escort people quickly out of the building.

All Jace wanted to do was find Lillian and make sure she wasn't harmed. But he knew she would want to make sure the building was secure first. That innocent people were safe. And while Jace didn't like that, he would respect her wishes. He had no doubt she'd paid a price to get that info to him. He wouldn't let it be wasted.

As they were escorting the last of the people from the building, he could hear Derek explaining on the phone what was happening to an obviously livid Congresswoman Glasneck.

"Glasneck refuses to cancel, so we're going to the emergency third location." Frustration was etched on Derek's face.

"I didn't even know there was a third location." And to be honest, he didn't care about the LESS Summit anymore. All Jace's attention was focused on getting to Lillian.

"The Clarke Building. An ordinary office building about three blocks away." Derek provided the address. "Small, unimpressive, nondescript. A conference room with no windows on the second floor. Opposite of what Glasneck wanted."

"I'm not coming, Derek. I've got to find Lily. She's in trouble." Jace respected the man but didn't care. What could Derek do, fire him? Even if this was his real job, Jace wouldn't care.

But Derek just nodded. "Find her. LESS is now going to be bare-bones anyway. The ceremony and pomp will have to be done some other way. This is just going to be Congresswoman Glasneck and a couple other key people flipping a switch." He provided a few more details about where they would be.

Jace was already taking off toward the lobby. "I'll report in as soon as I know something about Lillian. And we'll get to you if we can."

He prayed they'd be able to.

The last of the civilians were being led out the main entrance and police were clearing all the protesters in the vicinity of city hall. Jace had already tried calling Lillian's phone a dozen times. Each time the call went straight to voice mail.

"Jace."

He turned to find Saul behind him. "Is your sector clear?"

Saul hesitated a second before nodding. "When last I checked."

"Okay, I think the building's clear, then."

Saul didn't give his usual grin, just nodded. "Good. I'm glad you figured out that there was a threat."

"It was all Lillian, she clued me in, even though I'm almost positive she was under duress. Have you seen her? Or Carnell?"

"Um, yeah, a while ago, before we started the evac. I think she was just getting here. Said something about having proof about Carnell."

"Yeah, that's what she told me, too. I'm sure Derek can use your help securing the new LESS location. The Clarke Building, two blocks east of here. It's bare-bones, most of the VIPs won't be a part of it now, but LESS is still going live."

Saul's lips thinned. "Okay, I'll head over there right now. I've just got one thing to do first."

Jace didn't know what could be more important than getting directly over to the summit, but he honestly didn't care. Protecting the summit was Derek's concern now. This building was clear and Jace was damn well going to find Lillian.

"Eakin!" Saul called as Jace ran toward the stairs. "When I saw her as she came in, Lillian mentioned something about the roof. I don't know if that's where she is, but maybe."

Jace gave a wave of acknowledgment but didn't slow down. As he turned the corner bringing him to the main stairwell, he had to make a decision. Up or down. If Saul was right and she was on the roof, Jace didn't want to waste time looking in the basement section.

He won't get the drop on me down here again.

Those had been Lillian's words. *Down here.*

Maybe she'd been heading toward the roof when Poniard saw her earlier, but she wasn't there now. Or at least hadn't been when she called him to get the people out of the building.

He headed down the stairs, memories of finding Lily's swinging form haunting him from the last time he'd taken these stairs. He prayed he wouldn't find something worse.

A few minutes of storming through rooms—even the ones behind the padlocked door—had Jace worried he'd made the wrong decision. Maybe she was up on the roof. He was about to make his way up there when he heard a sound coming from the supply closet—like a call for help.

But Jace knew before he even opened the door that couldn't be right, the sound was from too far away to be coming from the supply closet.

He reached for the handle and found it locked. That was strange. It hadn't been locked as they were securing the building the past two days.

He heard the sound again—a muffled male yell—and stepped back to kick in the door. The door flew from its hinges when his foot hit it and opened.

Nothing. Nobody bound and gagged, like he expected.

He wiped a hand over his eyes. Wishful thinking. The stress was getting to him. Obviously the sound couldn't be from here.

He would check the roof, since he'd already checked every possible room in the basement.

But as he was closing the door he heard it again. Jace's head jerked up. That damn well hadn't been wishful thinking or stress. That had been a yell for help. And it had been coming from right in front of him. Right through the wall. A wall that should lead nowhere, according to the building plans he'd studied extensively.

Jace immediately began knocking against the far wall, more frantically, when he heard the yell again.

"Who's there? Keep yelling," Jace yelled back. When he moved a shelving unit he saw the hole. Doubling his efforts, he threw the shelf to the side and crawled through the hole.

What the hell?

"Help. Please."

The voice was becoming weaker.

"I'm here. Keep yelling."

"Eakin? We're here. Help us. Hurry."

"Carnell?" What the hell was going on? Jace moved farther into the large room. What was this? "Where are you?"

"Here. God, hurry, Eakin. There's a bomb."

Jace ran toward Carnell's voice and found him tied up in an adjoining room. Bleeding heavily.

Lillian was tied up and gagged next to him.

Very much alive. She was not only alive, but had also somehow gotten her pocketknife out and, with her own wrists secured behind her back, was attempting to cut through Carnell's tied hands. She'd already gotten his gag out, and would've had them both untied before too long.

Jace glanced at the explosive device. But maybe not fast enough.

"You're hurt," Jace said to Philip before diving down to help Lillian.

"I'll be fine. Thank God you're here," Philip said as Jace cut through Lillian's bonds first then did the same to Philip's. "We've got to get everyone out of here. That bomb is set to go off in less than twenty minutes."

"We've already evacuated the building."

As soon as her hands were free, Lillian reached up and pulled the gag out of her mouth. "You understood. Thank God."

Jace reached over and cupped the back of her neck, pulling her forehead against his. "Mentioning Daryl was smart. Clued me in immediately."

"It was my only option," she whispered. "Poniard was torturing Philip. Threatening to grab a mom and kid—"

"Poniard? Poniard is the mole?" Jace let out a blistering curse. "I just saw him. He was acting a little weird, but everything was already crazy with the evacuation."

"Thank God you stopped the summit," Philip said as Jace got Lillian to her feet and helped him stand. "I didn't even get to the part that sent me down here in the first place. The much worse part."

Phillip looked from Lillian to Jace.

"What?" they both demanded at the same time.

"You know how Saul has been traveling to police stations all over the country for the last eight months to help with the setup of the LESS system? What he conveniently failed to mention was that he also rigged those stations with biological weapons. If LESS had gone live today, Saul had rigged it so the connecting systems all over the country would've released the biological hazard. The death toll would've been in the thousands, maybe tens of thousands. All law enforcement."

Lillian's ugly curse was the exact sentiment Jace was feeling. And she didn't even know the half of it.

"That's a pretty big problem," Jace said. "Because we got this building clear, but the summit is still on at a different location. And I just told Poniard where it's being held."

Chapter Nineteen

Jace was reaching for his cell phone before he finished his sentence. He immediately cursed before putting it away.

"No signal. Poniard had to figure I would eventually end up down here. He probably set up some sort of jammer."

Jace and Lillian both ran over to the bomb. "We've got to get this thing disarmed," she said. "If the building comes down, there's no way there won't be complete panic outside."

"I'll take care of the bomb. You guys have to get over to the summit and stop Poniard." Jace told them where the summit had been moved to, then began studying the explosive device more closely.

Lillian's gut clenched. "Jace, there's no way for you to call for backup. For you to get the bomb squad in here. You'll be completely on your own."

Jace stood, wrapped his hands on either side

of her face and brought her in for a hard, quick kiss. "There's no time for them to get here even if I could get a call out. Law enforcement is maxed out outside. We're on our own."

Lillian grabbed his wrists and kissed him again. They both had jobs to do. He was trusting her to do hers, and she had to trust him to do his. "Then I'll see you soon. You damn well better make it out of this."

His grin sent heat to her core. Almost enough to melt the ice of fear surrounding her for him. "Bet on it."

He let her go and turned back to the explosive device. Lillian studied Philip. "We're going to have to move fast. Can you make it?"

"I have to. I'm the only one who can get LESS shut down in time to stop it from killing thousands of people."

They were through the passageway, out of the building and running into the Denver streets as fast as the crowds would let them. Backing people away from the City and County Building had just made the other areas more crowded. The sounds of chants and jeers were nearly deafening.

Lillian cleared a path for Philip, who was looking more and more pale. But he was right, they didn't have any choice: he had to make it.

She had a new respect for the determination in his eyes.

They finally made it to the small, almost unnoticeable building between two much taller ones. This was everything Congresswoman Glasneck *hadn't* wanted for the LESS Summit.

Not knowing the building specifics put Lillian at a tactical disadvantage, but Saul hadn't known about this backup location, either, so he couldn't have left them many surprises.

"We've got less than fifteen minutes," Philip said as they made it inside. "And we can't just go barging in. Saul has had this set up for months. He's only waited for the LESS Summit because he wanted to have these law-enforcement offices and stations around the country to be as crowded as possible. All he has to do is flip the switch to make LESS live, then start the computer program that opens the containers. He's probably already got it saved to a single keystroke. That's what I would do."

Lillian let out a string of curses. "So you're saying if we knock the door down and shoot him, he still might have a chance to put the program in motion and release the biological weapons."

"Exactly. I'll bet you any amount of money he's walking around with either a keyboard or a phone. Either can be used as his trigger. All he needs is a second to end the lives of thousands of people."

"Okay, then I'll knock the phone or keyboard out of his hand."

Philip shook his head. "That buys you time, but not much. He has a timing device as a backup plan. That's how I stumbled onto this whole thing to begin with, the countdown. Once LESS goes live, one minute afterward the canisters will release."

This just kept getting worse. "Can you stop it?"

"Yes. If I can access Poniard's digital trigger, whether it's a phone or a computer, I can stop it. I'll have to work the system backward, but I can do it."

"In under a minute?" Lillian tried to keep the incredulity out of her voice, but failed.

"You have your gifts, Muir. I have mine."

Lillian nodded at him. "I owe you an apology." For more than just accusing him of being the mole. For the way she'd treated him—like he wasn't good enough to truly be on the team. Now he was standing in a puddle of his own blood, ready to fight in the best way he knew how. It was all anyone could ask.

Maybe Philip wasn't such a jackass after all.

"Later, Muir. I don't have time for female hysterics or teary heartfelt hugs."

Or maybe he was.

Lillian notified the extra security guards of the problem and set them up outside the conference room door, ready to breach on her mark. She quickly explained the danger of rushing in too soon.

Since the summit had been downscaled, the only security out here was private sector and Denver local PD. Any Secret Service agents who'd been assigned here were in the closed conference room with Congresswoman Glasneck. Derek was in there, too. All of them could be counted on to take out Saul, but not if they didn't know Saul was the traitor.

And Saul would be waiting for someone to come through this door. Would be ready for that.

"Lillian, we've got less than ten minutes until LESS is scheduled to go live."

"Turn on your comm unit," she told him. "Be ready to burst in with the security team. I'll get the trigger away from Poniard, and then you'll work your magic."

"This is the only door. There's no windows. How are you going to get into the room?"

"You have your gifts, I have mine, Carnell. And right now mine includes my size."

Less than a minute later one of the security guards was giving her a boost up to the industrial-size air-conditioning vent. Lillian belly-crawled as quickly as she could through the small ductwork without making noise.

Arriving at the square grate over the room took longer than she wanted, and then she cursed when she found the situation to be even worse than she'd thought. Things had already escalated.

A Secret Service agent, most probably dead by the amount of blood lost from the bullet wound in his neck, was lying slumped over in the corner. Lillian shifted to be able to see the other side of the room better, and her breath caught in her throat. Derek had been shot also, perhaps multiple times. A man in a suit was holding a balled-up shirt against Derek's thigh, and blood was running unchecked from his shoulder.

Saul Poniard was pacing back and forth. "The current state of law enforcement is a laughingstock. Surely you can see that by re-setting the baseline I am doing this country a great favor. Something that is needed."

"By killing innocent people?" Congress-woman Glasneck asked. She was over against the south wall, huddled with half a dozen other people.

"The price of liberty is sometimes death itself. Plus, these people are not innocent, they are part of the problem."

"And us, Saul?" Glasneck asked again. "I've been working with you for months. Are you going to kill everyone in this room also?"

"I will not be deterred from what I am meant to do. It is my destiny. Individual lives are not what matter. Change is what matters."

Lillian looked at her watch. Four minutes. Four minutes until LESS was scheduled to go live and the bomb at the City and County Building was set to detonate. She couldn't even allow herself to think about Jace. She trusted him to be able to do what he needed to do.

"They'll know it's you." An older, heavyset man next to the congresswoman glared at Saul. "Do you think you're going to get away with this? That no one is going to notice a room full of dead people, including a congresswoman?"

"I think there's going to be enough chaos in just a few minutes to leave everyone in utter confusion. The lives of half a dozen will be of very little consequence in the bigger picture. And out of the confusion, I will rise up and lead. Lead law enforcement to the greatness it can be. To reset the path of this country the way it needs to be reset."

Saul's voice was rising with his passion. Lillian used the noise to speak into the comm unit.

"Philip," she whispered. "Poniard's got a phone in his hand, like you said. Gun in the other one. He's ready for an ambush through the door, so make sure everyone stands down."

"Roger that. But we're out of time, Lillian. Less than three minutes."

Saul was still yelling at the people huddled against the wall. "And never again will someone like me—someone with vision, focus and purpose—be denied the chance to serve in whatever capacity they see fit. To be a part of the most elite. Never again will I be rejected. For years, Omega Sector thought I wasn't capable of being on their precious SWAT team. Unfortunately, they'll all be dead, so I won't be able to gloat in their faces that I'm smarter than them."

Spittle flew across the room as he said it. Lillian barely refrained from rolling her eyes. This was all about Saul being jealous because he didn't make the SWAT team?

"Lil, once LESS goes live, the one-minute countdown is on, no matter what," Philip reminded her in her ear. "You've got to take him."

Philip was right. Lillian was treating this like a normal hostage situation, where she could just wait out the perp. Eventually he'd tire himself out and lower his weapon or become complacent.

They didn't have that kind of time now.

As Saul continued his rant, Lillian silently moved the grate that covered the vent opening, progressing slowly but with purpose.

"Thirty seconds until LESS goes live."

Lillian said a quick prayer that Jace had gotten the bomb disabled. They'd know for sure in just a few seconds. Saul would, too, and once he did, he wouldn't hesitate to immediately release the biological weapons all over the country.

Lillian waited until he crossed under her again, then forgot all about quiet and yanked the grate up and dove out of the opening, headfirst, landing on top of Saul.

Her training said to get the gun out of his right hand, but she pried the phone from his left hand instead. Keeping him from triggering the canisters was most important.

She was able to get the phone out of Saul's hand. She was too close for him to shoot, but she grunted when he hit her with his gun, barely missing her head and grazing her shoulder. Damn it, this bastard had hit her with that gun enough times for one day.

Keeping the phone out of his reach, she used her momentum to roll both of them forward, bringing her elbow up to catch him in the jaw. She jumped to her feet and grabbed Saul by the shirt, pulling his back off the floor. She slammed her fist into his nose, hearing the crack as it broke under her force.

"It just went live, Lillian. LESS just went live!" Philip's voice shouted into her ear.

One minute. That was all the time they had left.

"Breach! I've got Saul's phone." She heard the door burst open behind her and turned to toss Philip the phone. The security force trained their weapons on Saul.

Still held up by her fist on his clothing, Saul began to laugh. "You're too late. That bomb in the City and County Building is nothing compared to what's coming."

Lillian glanced over. "Philip?"

Philip didn't look up as his fingers typed rapidly on Saul's phone. "Working voodoo now. Do not disturb."

She brought Saul closer to her face. "Philip found out about your canisters and knows how to stop them."

Saul's face mottled in fury. "Don't do it, Carnell. Omega Sector is just using you. You know how elitist they are. We can be a part of something new. Better."

"New and better by killing tens of thousands of people?" She brought her fist into his jaw again. "Shut up."

Saul spat blood. "Philip. You know I'm telling the truth. Omega's best-of-the-best crap? According to who? The wrong people are making the decisions. It's time for a change."

Philip walked over to them. "You know what? You're right, Saul, it *is* time for a change."

"Philip." Damn it. Philip couldn't let Saul get into his head now. There were only seconds left. "Don't let him…"

Philip dropped the phone on the floor next to Saul. "But not your way. Law enforcement, Omega Sector included, needs to take a good long look at itself. Make the needed changes. I want to be a part of that. But not your way." Philip turned to Lillian. "I did it. The connection to the canisters has been severed. It's safe."

Saul jerked away from Lillian and made a tackle for Philip, but Philip was ready. It was his fist that hit Saul this time. Saul fell to the floor, moaning.

Lillian nodded at Philip as the guards handcuffed Saul and led him away. One was already on a radio, calling in an ambulance for Derek. Lillian rushed over to him where he was propped against the wall. Congresswoman Glasneck joined her at his side.

"Derek?" His normally tan skin was devoid of all color. He was so still, Lillian reached up to take his pulse. "Wake up."

"I'm awake," Derek muttered. "You did good, Lily."

"Excuse me, but you're not allowed to call me that." Only Jace was. "Don't think that just because you've successfully gotten yourself shot twice, I'm going to let you call me anything short of my full name."

She said it jokingly as she removed the shirt covering the wound on Derek's thigh to glance at it.

"How bad?" he muttered, eyes closed.

He knew she wouldn't lie. "Not life-threatening." Unless he kept bleeding. "But bad enough that you need to be taken straight to the hospital."

Derek nodded, then leaned farther back against the wall.

"I have to go check on Jace. We had to leave him with the explosive device in city hall. Poniard had set it up so the explosion would happen the same time the canisters were released. Maximum chaos and damage. There hasn't been an explosion, so I'm assuming he took care of it." Thank God.

Congresswoman Glasneck stood when Lillian did. "Thank you. I had no idea Saul Poniard was capable of such treachery."

Lillian gave a half shrug. "He was convinced

of the rightness of his own actions. I hope the LESS system can still be utilized."

Glasneck shook her head sadly. "Maybe one day, but not right now. If there's anything I've become convinced of in the last hour, it's that although connecting all law-enforcement systems may help fight crime, it also allows for law enforcement as a whole to be attacked rather easily. You bring down LESS, and it can do countrywide damage."

Lillian gave the congresswoman a nod and then turned to jog out the door. She gave Philip—who was now sitting on the floor looking exhausted—a nod and continued past him when he gave her a small salute. Saul was loudly explaining his intentions and proclaiming his innocence to the guards who had taken him into custody. Lillian ignored him completely. She'd heard more than enough out of him today.

Outside, the local police were still clearing the area, keeping demonstrators back from the buildings. She saw her teammate Ashton Fitzgerald helping with crowd control and made her way over to him. She explained what had happened with Saul and Derek.

"Do I need to get in there to help Derek?" Ashton had to shout to be heard over the roar of the crowd.

"No, just make sure the paramedics can get to him. You're needed out here. Have you seen Jace?"

"No. Cell-phone coverage is still down, and honestly we can't do anything until we clear this crowd out."

Lillian nodded. "I'm going to check on him and then I'll be back." She had to see with her own eyes to make sure Jace was okay.

Ashton nodded. "Okay. Comms aren't worth a damn out here, either, with the noise level. So just find me when you're back."

Lillian sprinted for the City and County Building. They needed as much help with crowd control as they could get. She entered the building and ran down the stairs toward the opening in the supply closet.

"Jace?" Nothing. "Eakin, you okay?"

She scurried through the hole, into the opening. "Jace! I just wanted to make sure you're okay."

She heard some sort of scuffle from farther back in a room, past where the explosive device had been placed. "Jace?"

Something was definitely not right. Had Jace hurt himself somehow after defusing the explosive device? Was someone else down here? Lillian pulled her sidearm, keeping it close to her chest.

The muffled sound came again and Lillian rushed into the far room. At the other end, near some sort of second entrance, stood Damien Freihof, a gagged-and-bound Jace in front of him.

He had a gun pointed directly at Jace's temple.

"Agent Muir," Freihof said, his smile large and wide. "I was wondering how long it would take before you came to look for Mr. Eakin."

Lillian's weapon was immediately pointed directly at Freihof. She didn't have a shot right now with Jace in front of him like a shield, but Jace wouldn't be anyone's human shield for long, particularly not Freihof's. Jace didn't seem to be hurt. When he made his move, Lillian would be ready.

She glanced at Jace's face, ready to read whatever it was he would want her to do.

The sheer agony she saw in his eyes caught her off guard.

"What the hell did you do, Freihof?" she whispered. Had he hurt Jace? There had to be some sort of terrible wound she couldn't see that was putting that look on his face.

"No need to be angry. As a matter of fact, everyone should be thanking me." Freihof's voice rang with childlike excitement. "I haven't done anything bad. As a matter of fact, all I did was stage a reunion between brothers!"

A reunion between bro—

"You remember Jace's brother, Daryl, don't you, Lillian?"

For the first time in her professional career, Lillian's weapon faltered as her own personal nightmare stepped out from the shadows beside her. Her hand began to shake as shock flooded her whole body. The Glock shook so greatly in her hand she could hardly keep hold of it.

"Hi, Lillian, baby. I've been looking for you for a long time." Daryl trailed a finger down her cheek. All she could do was stare at him.

His fist crashed into her face and Lillian let the blessed blackness consume her.

Chapter Twenty

As soon as Daryl's fist flew toward Lillian, Jace dove at them. Freihof was expecting it and just laughed, grabbed Jace and pulled him away. He watched, helpless, as Lillian fell to the floor.

"Brother dearest seems pretty excited to see your girlfriend," Freihof whispered in his ear. "He told me a little about what happened between them. Don't you just love a classic romance?"

Jace dove toward them again as Daryl crouched down to stroke Lily's face. She was already regaining consciousness. Freihof grabbed Jace and threw him to his knees, clocking him against the back of his neck with the gun. Jace ignored the pain, yelling at Daryl through the tape.

"I think your brother wants to talk to you, Daryl." Freihof ripped the tape off Jace's mouth.

"Don't you touch her, Daryl. Keep your damn hands off her."

Lillian was moaning on the floor, still having not quite woken up. It wasn't because Daryl had hit her that hard. Lily could take a punch. It was because her brain didn't want her to wake up. Didn't want to force her into trauma she wasn't ready for.

Daryl now looked as evil on the outside as he was on the inside. Burns covered over half his face and trailed down his neck before they were cut off by his T-shirt.

"I can't believe you would choose her over your own flesh and blood, *brother*," Daryl spat out. "She left me in that warehouse to die."

"We both know why. What you did to her." If Jace could reach his brother right now, he would rip him apart limb by limb.

"I had that warehouse ready to blow up," Daryl scoffed. "I knew the cops were closing in. I had been stupid to move into trafficking. Even had a body that looked sort of like mine. Some dealer from across the border who happened to be the same height and weight as me."

Jace sucked in a breath as Daryl stood. He pushed Lillian with the toe of his boot but didn't do anything further. "Lillian was the one who was supposed to be in that fire, not me. Fortunately one of my guys came in and dragged me out after she clocked me over the head with that bottle. The rest of our scheme went as planned. He identified my 'body' to the police. Then we took off."

Lillian gave a pitiful moan, her head tossing back and forth. She'd be waking up soon. Waking up to a nightmare.

Daryl nudged her again with his foot. "I looked for her. All over Tulsa, then even farther. Never dreamed she'd join law enforcement, as pathetic as she was. But she won't be any good to anyone—especially law enforcement—once I'm through with her."

Lillian's eyes opened at that moment. Bile rose in Jace's throat as a look of terror blanketed her features. Almost immediately she was shaking again, her brown eyes darting all around.

"Lillian, look at me, baby," he whispered, trying to eliminate the desperation from his tone. Her eyes continued to dart from place to place, her rapid, shallow breathing causing her to shake further.

"Tiger Lily." He kept his tone firm. Calm. Banished every bit of fear and panic threatening to bubble up from inside him. "It's Jace. I'm here with you. I'm here with you, and you're going to be okay."

Her eyes finally rested on him. "Jace?"

He would give every cent he owned to never see this look of terror and helplessness cross

Lillian's face ever again. "I'm here, sweetheart. With you. I'm here."

"You're here." Her words were weak, but her breathing slowed just enough that he stopped worrying that she would pass out again. He nodded at her, keeping their eyes locked.

A roar erupted from him as Daryl reached down and snatched her up by her hair, yanking her face back. "Guess what, I'm here, too, bitch!" Daryl backhanded her and she fell hard to the floor.

This time, she didn't pass out. This time her small hand tightened into a fist.

That's right, sweetheart. Find your fight.

Daryl was weak, pudgy. Lillian was capable of taking him down in under ten seconds. Her mind just had to believe that she could. She sat back up, her eyes finding Jace's again. They were still laced with fear, but her breathing was more under control. If Daryl kept pushing, he was eventually going to find that Lillian could now push back.

Much, much harder.

"That's right, Tiger Lily. You just take a minute and remember who you are. What you can do."

"Stop talking to her!" Daryl screamed, shoving her again.

Her other hand was clenching into a fist now,

too. Jace tensed his muscles, trying to balance himself more fully, ready to throw himself backward at Freihof when Lillian completely woke up and made her move. It wouldn't be long.

But then Daryl stopped yelling. Stopped the violence. He dropped behind Lillian, wrapping his arm around her shoulder, pulling her back up against his chest.

Eyes so much like Jace's own looked back at him as Daryl trailed his fingers up and down Lillian's throat and cheek from behind. "You two were so inseparable when you were kids. Like she was your family instead of me. Like I hadn't raised you and given you everything."

"You raised me in a gang and had me performing illegal activities before I was a teenager."

"You got to go to school. Got to eat three square meals a day. Had clothes and money when you needed it. And then you met Lillian and everything changed. Everything became about her. All I wanted was my brother back."

Lillian was frozen in Daryl's embrace.

"Let her go, Daryl. You can have me back. We can do whatever you want, we'll make it work."

Daryl snuggled in closer to Lillian's neck, breathing in her scent. "Did I ever tell you how sweetly she begged? Begged me to spare your life? Begged me not to put her back in the closet where I kept her. Begged me not to hurt her. She was so good at it."

Daryl nuzzled her neck, then forced her head back and kissed her.

Jace prayed she would come out swinging, that she would use one of the hundreds of ways she knew to break out of Daryl's embrace.

But as soon as Daryl moved away from her, Jace recognized that blank stare. Pain and violence had scared her but kept her present. She would eventually have fought back.

But not from this. Just like the other night, Lillian had completely shut down. Her brain had disassociated, was keeping her conscious mind at a distance.

She wasn't feeling any fear, but this Lillian was helpless. Not able to fight, not able to provide any tactical assistance to help get them out of here. There was no way Jace could fight both Daryl with his knife and Freihof with his gun, especially bound like he was.

"I think I'd like to hear you beg again." Daryl leaned away from her, pushing at her, obviously expecting hysteria and fear like before. But Lillian just looked at him with wide eyes, almost like she was a child.

No fear. No pain. But also no fight.

Daryl didn't have the insight to realize what was going on with Lillian, but Freihof did. "Interesting," he said quietly from behind Jace. "Disassociation."

"What are you looking at?" Daryl finally said when Lillian just continued to stare at him blankly. He slapped her, and her head fell to the side. She blinked but then looked back up at Daryl like she was waiting for him to tell her what to do.

Jace began to struggle more frantically against the duct tape that bound his hands behind his back. Lillian frightened and shaking had been nauseating to watch.

Lillian utterly defenseless was beyond terrifying.

Daryl stood and yanked her up by her tactical vest. At her continued blank stare he pulled her right up to his face. "Not scared anymore?"

His mouth covered hers in what would've technically been described as a kiss, but was really meant to be a device of pain and dominance. On any other given day, under other circumstances, Lillian would've kicked him on his ass.

Now her hands just came up and weakly rested on Daryl's shoulders. Just like they had on Jace's in bed when she blanked out. She wasn't kissing him, but she wasn't pushing Daryl away, either.

"Lily! Come on, baby. Come back to me," Jace called out.

Daryl stepped back, smirking at Jace, keeping an arm wrapped around her limp shoulders. "I've been waiting a lot of years to find sweet Lillian here. To remind her whom she belongs to. When Damien found me a few days ago and told me he knew where she was—where both of you were—I knew I couldn't miss the chance. To get her back. To make her pay for this." He gestured to the scars that ravaged most of his face.

Jace ignored him. "Lillian, come on, sweetheart…" She just continued to stare blankly ahead.

"I'll admit I thought it would be a little harder. Thought I might have to kill you both outright." Daryl pulled out a knife. "But now it looks like I'll just take Lillian with me. I'll find a nice cage to put her back in and take her out when I want to play with her."

Daryl held the knife right in front of Lillian's face like it was a toy. "That okay with you, little pet? Ready to be my dog?"

Jace lunged for Daryl again as he took the knife and made a shallow cut along the side of Lillian's neck. Freihof grabbed him and pulled him back, but Jace immediately lunged again as Daryl made another small cut and Lillian didn't move.

Freihof's pistol came down on the base of Jace's skull again, making him sink to the floor. Through the haze he heard Freihof chuckling. "I realize this might be the pot calling the kettle black, but your brother is pretty sick. I never knew I'd be getting such entertainment when I brought him here."

Jace looked up, fighting back blackness, to look at Lillian again. "C'mon, baby. Fight for me, Tiger Lily. I love you." Her blank brown eyes stared out at him.

Daryl moved away from her and walked over to stand in front of him. "She'll be coming with me. But you, baby brother, you're just a loose end that needs to be tied up. I guess I'll finally need to finish what I threatened to start twelve years ago."

No emotion crossed Daryl's face as he stabbed the knife through Jace's shoulder. The force threw him back, but Daryl grabbed him by the hair and twisted the knife. Agony flooded through Jace.

"That's for the fact that you would've chosen her over your own flesh and blood all those years ago." He pulled out the knife and brought it to Jace's throat. "And this is for the fact that you would still choose her today. Even as broken as she obviously is."

Chapter Twenty-One

The fog was soft and cloudlike all around her. Gentle, yet permeating. Time moved differently here. More slowly. She didn't have to worry about all the things waiting for her on the outside. She could just stay here, where no one could hurt her. Where there would be nothing left to remember when the fog finally lifted. Just blessed numbness.

But even as she clung to the fog—the only darkness she'd ever known that wouldn't hurt her—something beat against her mind. The knowledge that something was different.

Lily.

The voice penetrated the fog. A good voice. Strong. A voice that would never hurt her. But she pushed it away. That voice didn't belong here. Nothing belonged here but the emptiness. The numbness.

Come back to me.

Lillian tried to melt further into the fog. Why

wouldn't this voice leave her alone? There were things outside the fog that would hurt her. If she followed the voice she knew pain waited at the other end.

Agony. Terror.

Fight for me.

She didn't want to go. Didn't want to face what was out there. Knew that the devil waited just beyond the fog. That if she faced him now, the fog would never protect her again.

She couldn't do it.

She felt the prick of pain in her neck at a distance. It didn't really hurt, not much. But she shouldn't feel it at all. The fog had never let anything in before. When the prick at her neck came again, Lillian tried to pull herself back more fully into the blessed darkness.

"Tiger Lily."

Jace. That voice was Jace's.

She didn't move. Didn't blink. Didn't breathe. But the fog began to sink away in layers.

Jace. Jace was here.

"I love you."

More of the fog slid away and she could see as well as hear.

Oh, God, it was Daryl. Daryl was here. He was alive. Her mind demanded that she go back into the fog. That if she stayed in the light, if she left the fog, she might never be whole again.

She couldn't risk it.

The fog fell back around her as Daryl turned away and walked over to stand in front of Jace. He said something that didn't penetrate her haze and then stabbed Jace in the shoulder.

Jace didn't yell, didn't beg or scream. But she could see the blood pouring from the wound as Daryl twisted the knife and pulled it back out.

And then he put the knife to Jace's throat.

No.

With that one thought, the fog fell completely away. It couldn't hold her if she wouldn't let it. As it left, terror and pain rolled over her, threatening to drown her in their enormity.

No.

She would not stand here protecting herself in numbness while the man she loved lost his life to the monster who had stolen so much from her.

She would not do nothing. Not now. Not ever again.

She sprang.

With all the rage of the eighteen-year-old who hadn't been able to protect herself, she *attacked*.

Neither Daryl nor Freihof was expecting any resistance from her. She was able to kick the knife out of Daryl's hand and away from Jace's throat, then used her momentum to propel herself around so her other leg swung out over Jace's head and connected with Freihof's gun, sending it flying across the room.

Daryl roared as he tackled her from behind, arms coming around her torso. Lillian didn't hesitate. She brought her head back full force against his face, breaking his nose, then swung her booted heel into his kneecap. Daryl screamed and released her.

Never again.

Freihof ran for his gun, but Jace threw himself at the other man, knocking them both onto the floor. She ran over to help Jace, who would never be able to defeat Freihof while wounded and without the use of his hands. Freihof quickly got back to his feet, about to kick Jace in the head, when Lillian leaped for him, knocking him away.

She wasted no time, striking Freihof with a fierce uppercut, then with a heel to his face broke her third nose of the day.

That's for Grace, you bastard.

As Freihof fell to the floor, Lillian leaped and spun, knowing Daryl would be back on her.

He was, knife in hand.

"Time to die, bitch. I should've done this a long time ago."

Daryl's voice—the voice of her nightmares—sent a sliver of fear through Lillian, but she pushed it away. He jabbed at her with the knife and she quickly stepped to the side to evade. But Daryl was expecting that and caught her with a punch to the jaw. The blow spun her head around.

"Remember my fist, sweetheart?" Daryl sneered. "Don't worry, I'm going to make sure you remember every part of me before you—"

Lillian didn't let him finish. She stepped back so she was out of the reach of the knife and brought her leg around in a flying round-house kick that caught him in the head. She followed it with a side kick that barreled into his chest, propelling him backward half a dozen feet.

She realized her mistake as soon as he hit the floor. He landed right where he'd taken her sidearm from her earlier. Daryl was going to have it in his hand before she could get to him.

"Lil…"

She heard the weak call from Jace on the other side of the room, then felt something hit her foot. He'd kicked Freihof's gun over to her.

Daryl swung his arm around with the gun in hand as she dropped and grabbed the weapon Jace had provided. She heard a gun fire, felt the recoil of her own. She waited for pain but felt none.

Daryl groaned as he fell back, his weapon

falling from his hand. She'd gotten off the shot. Hit him in the chest.

She ran over, kicking the gun away, but she needn't have bothered.

Daryl was dead. For good this time. Checking his pulse confirmed it.

Lillian brought her weapon back around to train it on Freihof. He was just as deadly. But he was no longer where she'd been fighting him, over by Jace. Instead he was at a back entrance to the room.

"I reset the bomb. Hope that's okay." He gave her a small salute. "Another time, Agent Muir. Give my regards to your colleagues."

He slipped out the door.

There was nothing Lillian wanted to do more than go after Freihof, but she couldn't.

Lillian ran over to Jace. He had lost a lot of blood from his shoulder wound. She grabbed the knife and cut through the tape binding his hands. "You're bleeding bad, Jace."

He nodded. "I know. But we've got to stop that bomb. Get me over there. I stopped it once, I can do it again."

Jace was shaky on his feet. She put his good arm around her shoulder and, taking as much of his weight as she could, led him back over to the explosive device. She held him upright, and with shaky hands he once again dismantled the bomb, with just seconds to spare.

"There," he said to the bomb when he was finished. "Stay dead this time."

"Exactly my feelings about Daryl." She kissed his shoulder as they both slid to the floor. "You got that gun to me just in time."

Jace gave her a smile, bringing his hand to her cheek. "You came back from where you were just in time."

"Because you called me back. It was you who got through the fog."

"I'll always call you back, Tiger Lily. Just like you do for me."

Lillian reached up to kiss him, but before she could, he collapsed to the floor.

Chapter Twenty-Two

It was touch-and-go for three days. The shoulder wound was bad enough, but it was the internal hemorrhaging from being clocked on the head that actually put Jace's life in danger. The surgeon had to drill an emergency hole in his skull to allow release of the pressure. Then he had to be kept in a medically induced coma to give his brain every opportunity to heal.

The time between Jace collapsing in her arms and when those blue eyes opened to look at her again were the longest three days of Lillian's life.

She hadn't left his side. Teammates had brought her clean clothes and food and necessities. Lillian wasn't leaving Jace alone.

Because she knew if the roles were reversed, he wouldn't leave her alone, either. She trusted that—trusted *Jace*—with every fiber of her being.

On the third day of Jace's coma, the day they

began waking him up, she sat holding his hand, staring at his face. Willing him with every bit of energy she had to open those blue eyes. The doctor had explained that it took each person a different amount of time to wake up. To find his or her way back to consciousness.

But, the doctor also had to warn, on rare occasions they never found their way back.

Jace would. He would find his way out of the fog. She would lead him, the way he'd led her.

She reached over and planted a kiss on his unmoving lips. "I'm here, Eakin. Find your way back to me."

A few hours later Jace still wasn't awake. The doctor had come by twice outside his usual rounds, and although she hadn't said anything negative, Lillian knew she was concerned.

Jace would find his way back to her. He had to.

Molly Humphries-Waterman wheeled her husband through the door in a wheelchair an hour later. Derek was still recovering from his gunshot wounds, but the prognosis was good. It was going to take physical therapy, but Derek would eventually be back to full speed.

But it was yet another member of the Omega Sector team down, thanks to Damien Freihof.

"How's he doing?" Derek asked as Molly went to get them coffee.

"Nothing yet." Lillian had Jace's hand in hers. "The doc says it takes different people different amounts of time to wake up."

"It won't be long. Eakin is strong. And even more, he has someone here waiting who is the most important thing in the world to him."

She reached over and brushed a small lock of hair off Jace's forehead, willing him to open his eyes.

"So you heard Saul Poniard made a full confession?"

She looked over at Derek. "No. I've pretty much just been here. I don't know what's going on."

"I'm sure Steve Drackett will be providing an update to you soon. But yeah, Poniard gave up his whole Manifesto of Change, parts of which had been discovered within the Omega system a couple of weeks ago. Saul had nicknamed himself Guy Fawkes."

"As in the guy who tried to blow up the British parliament?"

"The very same."

Lillian rolled her eyes. "I have to admit, I never saw it. Never really looked past his surfer-boy grin."

"Poniard was setting you up for the fall, Lillian. Making it look like you set up both the explosive device in the City and County Building and the biological weapon canisters that would've gone live with LESS."

"I never dreamed Poniard hated me that much."

Derek shrugged. "Honestly, I don't think he did. I think you were an easy target. No family, no close friends. A loner."

"Someone easy to set up."

Derek smiled. "Not as easy as he and Freihof thought."

"Freihof got away." Frustration still ate at her. She'd been so close to taking him down.

"But with Saul out of the picture we've crippled Freihof in a lot of ways, including the broken nose you gave him. Plus, Ren McClement says there's been some new developments. We'll be hearing more about that soon, I'm sure."

"Good."

"And Daryl Eakin is dead. I know you know that."

Lillian hadn't told Derek many specifics about what had happened in the past with Daryl, but Derek knew it hadn't been good.

She nodded. "I got a second chance to fight my own personal monster, and this time I won. Not everybody gets that sort of second chance."

Derek pointed at Jace. "That man loves you. He would fight your monsters for you."

"I know, but—"

She stopped her sentence as Jace's voice interrupted her from the bed, husky and low. "No. I wouldn't fight your monsters. You can do that yourself. But I'll stand with you as you fight them. Every single time."

Lillian leaped over to him, cupping his cheeks. "That's even better." She smiled, kissing him as she stared into those blue eyes. "Hi. You found your way back to me."

"I always will. No matter how long it takes, I always will."

They would always find their way back to each other.

LILLIAN SLEPT IN the hospital bed with Jace that night.

Maybe he'd been slow to initially come out of the coma, but once he started Jace made much faster progress than was expected. Within a few hours he was sitting up with no dizziness and not long afterward was even taking steps by himself.

Different members of Omega Sector had come by all day to check on them and Derek. To shake Jace's hand and hug Lillian tight. To thank them for a job well done. Even Philip came by, finally stitched up from the wounds

Saul had given him. He even smiled and spoke without making anyone mad.

The traitor who had resided inside their family was now gone. Freihof would fall next.

The last visitor was someone Lillian hadn't ever talked to directly in person, but knew about. Ren McClement. Omega's most revered and somewhat notorious agent. In his midforties with brown hair and dark eyes that looked like they never missed a thing.

Rumors were that McClement's specialty was undercover ops. Long-term assignments. The ones no one with family or friends would take. McClement answered to very few people and always got his man, no matter what the cost.

The only thing that people agreed on about Ren McClement was that no one really knew him.

Except Jace. Evidently Jace knew him, given how the two embraced with a strong hug before Ren ruffled Jace's hair.

"Nearly dead wasn't what I was expecting when I brought you on for this mission, Eakin," Ren said as he sat down in the chair on the other side of Jace's bed from Lillian and nodded at her. "Agent Muir."

"Lillian, please."

She enjoyed watching the two men banter

with each other for the next couple of hours. Despite insults thrown on both sides, the respect the men had for each other all but permeated the air. Both of them made a point to draw her into the conversation as much as possible.

"I'm glad you two are okay," Ren said. "Your dead brother showing up was…unexpected."

Jace's eyes met hers. "Yeah, for all of us." He turned to Ren. "I'm sorry Freihof got away."

"Well, speaking of dead people being alive, we've had a pretty big development when it comes to Freihof."

"How so?" Lillian asked. She wanted Freihof behind bars so badly she could taste it.

"Evidently Natalie Freihof, Damien's beloved wife whose death is the very reason he's been taking his revenge on Omega Sector, is actually alive."

"What?" Jace and Lillian both said it at the same time.

"Yep. We're not sure if she's working with Freihof or not, but we're going to find out. I *personally* am going to find out."

Ren's dark eyes were so cold Lillian felt a little sympathy for the woman she'd never met.

"Whether she's working with him or not, his obsession with her is the key to drawing him out and trapping him. One way or another she'll help us bring Freihof down. I'll see to it."

Collateral damage sometimes happened in battles like this. But Freihof had to be stopped. If this dead wife could help, Lillian wouldn't argue against it.

"But this is all on me now," Ren said. "You two are just supposed to heal. Jace, I'm sure Steve Drackett's going to be in here any minute now asking you to join the Omega team permanently."

Jace smiled. "Nope, not for me. All I want is to get to my ranch and get it started. I'm out of this game for good."

Ren smiled. "Since your ranch just happens to be forty miles from Omega HQ, I'm sure Steve may still call on your services from time to time."

"I'm thankful for many reasons that my ranch is only forty miles from Omega." Jace turned to Lillian, heat clear in his eyes. "But none of them have a damn thing to do with Steve Drackett."

In the evening after everyone was gone, Lillian settled down in the uncomfortable lounge chair next to Jace, ready to try to get some rest.

She heard the bed shift and the next minute Jace's arms were scooping under her and tucking her in beside him. He lifted her as if he hadn't been stabbed and in a medically induced coma just a few hours earlier.

"Pretty sure heavy lifting isn't a good plan, Eakin," she said, but snuggled into his chest.

"First, not even under the most absurd of circumstance could you be considered heavy lifting. Second, you sleep next to me. Every night from here on out."

She didn't try to move away. There wasn't anywhere she wanted to be besides right next to him. But she couldn't just let his words slide. She had to make sure he knew what he was in for.

"I'm still broken," she whispered. "I know I made it back from the darkness and fought Daryl, but that doesn't end the nightmare for me. There are parts of me that…might never work correctly again. I'm permanently broken, Jace."

She felt his hand slide over her hair. "I've worked with the most elite soldiers in the world and can say that you are stronger and more capable than anybody I've ever known."

"Daryl almost won. I didn't even fight. If you hadn't found a way to call me back…"

His lips rested against her temple. "But you did fight. You fought your way out of the darkness and then you fought Daryl and won. You kept Freihof from killing me and thousands of innocent people."

"My PTSD can get pretty bad. I just want to

make sure you know what you're getting into. Before you start saying things like *forever*."

"Then I'm glad I'm about to have a ranch full of animals specifically for people like you."

"I thought you were supposed to be helping soldiers."

"It's for people who need time to put themselves back together. That includes you."

She wrapped her arm around his waist and threw a leg over his hips. "I can't promise I'm ever going to be normal. That I'll ever be like other women."

His thumb reached down and tilted her chin up so he could kiss her. "Thank God. I wouldn't want you any other way than what you are."

"Then you better hurry up and heal so I can get you home and back into a real bed."

"I don't care what bed we're in as long as every day that I wake up, you're in it with me. We have twelve years to make up for. And everything else we'll work through."

"I can't leave my job with Omega."

He laughed. "I wouldn't dare even try to suggest it. It's more than just your job. They're your family."

"You are, too. You always have been."

"And I always will be."

* * * * *

Look for the next book in USA TODAY
bestselling author Janie Crouch's
OMEGA SECTOR: UNDER SIEGE
miniseries,
IN THE LAWMAN'S PROTECTION,
available next month.

*And don't miss the previous books
in the series:*

DADDY DEFENDER
PROTECTOR'S INSTINCT
CEASE FIRE
MAJOR CRIMES

Available now from Harlequin Intrigue!

Get 4 FREE REWARDS!

We'll send you 2 FREE Books plus 2 FREE Mystery Gifts.

Harlequin® Romantic Suspense books feature heart-racing sensuality and the promise of a sweeping romance set against the backdrop of suspense.

FREE
Value Over
$20

YES! Please send me 2 FREE Harlequin® Romantic Suspense novels and my 2 FREE gifts (gifts are worth about $10 retail). After receiving them, if I don't wish to receive any more books, I can return the shipping statement marked "cancel." If I don't cancel, I will receive 4 brand-new novels every month and be billed just $4.99 per book in the U.S. or $5.74 per book in Canada. That's a savings of at least 12% off the cover price! It's quite a bargain! Shipping and handling is just 50¢ per book in the U.S. and 75¢ per book in Canada*. I understand that accepting the 2 free books and gifts places me under no obligation to buy anything. I can always return a shipment and cancel at any time. The free books and gifts are mine to keep no matter what I decide.

240/340 HDN GMYZ

Name (please print)

Address   Apt. #

City   State/Province   Zip/Postal Code

Mail to the **Reader Service**:
IN U.S.A.: P.O. Box 1341, Buffalo, NY 14240-8531
IN CANADA: P.O. Box 603, Fort Erie, Ontario L2A 5X3

Want to try two free books from another series? Call 1-800-873-8635 or visit www.ReaderService.com.

Get 4 FREE REWARDS!

We'll send you 2 FREE Books plus 2 FREE Mystery Gifts.

Harlequin Presents® books feature a sensational and sophisticated world of international romance where sinfully tempting heroes ignite passion.

FREE
Value Over
$20